DAMASO CLAIMS HIS HEIR

BY
ANNIE WEST

MILLS
BOON

Published in Great Britain 2014
by Mills & Boon, an imprint of Harlequin (UK) Limited,
Eton House, 18-24 Paradise Road, Richmond, Surrey, TW9 1SR

© 2014 Annie West

ISBN: 978-0-263-90895-4

Harlequin (UK) Limited's policy is to use papers that are natural,
renewable and recyclable products and made from wood grown in
sustainable forests. The logging and manufacturing processes conform
to the legal environmental regulations of the country of origin.

Printed and bound in Spain
by Blackprint CPI, Barcelona

Annie West has devoted her life to an intensive study of tall, dark, charismatic heroes who cause the best kind of trouble in the lives of their heroines. As a sideline she's also researched dream-worthy locations for romance, from bustling, vibrant cities to desert encampments and fairytale castles. It's hard work, but she loves a challenge. Annie lives with her family at beautiful Lake Macquarie, on Australia's east coast. She loves to hear from readers and you can contact her at www.annie-west.com or at PO Box 1041, Warners Bay, NSW 2282, Australia.

Recent titles by the same author:

AN ENTICING DEBT TO PAY *(At His Service)*
IMPRISONED BY A VOW
CAPTIVE IN THE SPOTLIGHT
DEFYING HER DESERT DUTY

For Ana Luisa Neves.
With heartfelt thanks for your patience and
Portuguese language expertise.

CHAPTER ONE

DAMASO SAW HER and his breath snagged in his lungs.

He who'd had women dancing to his tune well before he made his first million.

How long since one had quickened his pulse? He'd known divas and duchesses, models and Madonnas. In the early days there'd been tourists by the armful, and one memorable tango dancer whose sinuous body and blatant sexuality had made his teenage self burn with need. None had affected him the way she did—without effort.

For the first time she was alone, not laughing with her coterie of men. He was surprised to see her crouched, photographing flowers on the rainforest floor. She was so engrossed, she didn't notice him.

That was new for Damaso. He'd grown used to being watched and avidly sought after.

It pricked him that she was oblivious to him while he was hyper-aware of her. It infuriated him that his eyes strayed to her time and again, yet she had done no more than gift him with the dazzling smile she awarded so indiscriminately.

Damaso moved closer, intrigued. Was she really unaware or was she trying to pique his curiosity? Did she know he preferred to be the hunter, not the prey?

Beautiful blondes were commonplace in his world. Yet from the first day, watching her radiant face as she'd emerged drenched but undaunted from white-water rafting, Damaso had felt something new. A spark of connection.

Was it her unbounded energy? The devilment in her eyes as she risked her pretty neck again and again? Or that sexy gurgle of laughter that clutched at his vitals? Perhaps it was the sheer courage of a woman that didn't baulk at any challenge on a trek designed to spark the jaded interest of the world's ultra-wealthy.

'Marisa. There you are. I looked for you everywhere.' Young Saltram blundered out of the undergrowth to stop beside her. A computer geek who looked about eighteen, yet was worth upwards of seven figures annually, he was like an over-grown puppy salivating over a bone.

Damaso's jaw tightened as Saltram ate her up with his eyes—his gaze lingering on the delectable peach ripeness of her backside as she squatted with her camera.

Damaso stirred, but stopped as she turned her head. From this angle he saw what Saltram couldn't: her deep breath, as if she'd mustered her patience before turning.

'Bradley! I haven't seen you for hours.' She gave the newcomer a blinding smile that seemed to stun him.

That didn't stop him reaching out to help her rise, though it was clear she didn't need assistance. Damaso had never seen a woman so agile or graceful.

Saltram closed his hand around her elbow and she smiled coquettishly up at the youth.

Amazingly, Damaso felt something stark scour his belly. His fingers twitched as he resisted the urge to march across and yank the boy away.

She was laughing, flirting now, not at all perturbed that Saltram was breathing down her cleavage.

She wore shorts and hiking boots and her toned legs drew Damaso's gaze like a banquet set before a beggar. He swallowed, tasting his own hunger and the sharp, pungent tang of green apples.

Scowling, he recognised it was her scent filling his nostrils. How could that be? Standing in the shadows, he was too far away to inhale her perfume.

She turned and let Saltram guide her down the track, her long ponytail swaying across her narrow back. For a week Damaso had wanted to stroke that shining fall of gold and discover if it was as soft as it looked.

Yet he'd kept his distance, tired of dealing with fractious women who wanted more than he was prepared to give.

But she wouldn't make demands, the voice of temptation whispered. *Except in bed.*

For Princess Marisa of Bengaria had a reputation with a capital R. Pampered from birth, living carelessly off inherited riches, she was a party girl extraordinaire. The tabloids branded her wilful, reckless and as far from a demure, virginal princess as it was possible to get.

Damaso had told himself he was sick of high-maintenance women. Yet a week in her vicinity had given him a new perspective. She might be feckless but she wasn't needy.

She'd flirted with every man on the trek. Except him. Heat drilled through his belly as the significance of that hit.

She was *exactly* what he needed. He had no interest in virgins. A little wildness would add spice to a short vacation liaison.

Damaso smiled as he sauntered down the track after her.

Marisa turned her face to the waterfall's spray, grateful for its cooling, damp mist in this sultry heat. Her blood pumped fast and her limbs felt stretched and shaky from fatigue and adrenalin as she clung to the cliff face.

Yes! This was what she wanted. To lose herself in the challenge of the moment. To put aside all the—

'Marisa! Over here!'

She turned her head. Bradley Saltram watched her

from a perch well away from the waterfall. His grin was triumphant.

'Hey, you did it! Great going.' Bradley had confided his fear of heights. Even his relatively straightforward climb was a momentous achievement. No wonder he wore full safety harness and had Juan, their guide, in close attendance. 'I knew you could do it.'

But it was hard meeting his bright eyes, almost febrile with excitement and pleasure.

A hammer blow struck her square in the chest and she clutched at her precarious handhold. When he smiled that way, with such triumph, she remembered another smile. So radiant it had been like watching the sun's reflection. Eyes so clear and brilliant they'd been like the summer sky. Happiness so infectious it had warmed her to the core.

Stefan had always been able to make her forget her misery with a smile and a joke and a plunge into adventure, making a nonsense of the joyless, disapproving world that trapped them.

Marisa blinked, turning away from the bright-eyed American who had no idea of the pain he'd evoked.

A lump the size of Bengaria's cold, grey royal palace settled in her chest, crushing the air from her lungs and choking her throat. Her breath was a desperate whistle of snatched air.

No! Not now. Not here.

She turned back to Bradley, pinning a smile on her features. 'I'll see you at the bottom. I just want to check out the falls.'

Bradley said something but she didn't hear it over the drumming pulse in her ears. Already she was moving, swinging easily up, shifting her weight as she found new foot- and hand-holds on the slick rock-face.

That was what she needed, to concentrate on the challenge and the demands of the moment. Push away everything but the numbness only physical exertion brought.

She was high now, higher than she'd intended. But the rhythm of the climb was addictive, blotting out even Juan's shouted warning.

The spray was stronger here, the rock not merely damp but running with water.

Marisa tuned in to the roar of the falls, revelling in the pounding rush of sound, as if it could cleanse her of emotion.

A little to the left and she'd be at the spot where legend had it one brave boy had made the impossible dive into the churning pool of water below.

She paused, temptation welling. Not to make a name for herself by a daredevil act, but to risk herself in the jaws of possible oblivion.

It wasn't that she wanted to die. But dicing with danger was as close as she'd come lately to living, to believing there might possibly be joy in her life again.

The world was terminally grey, except in those moments when the agony of grief and loneliness grew piercingly vivid. Those moments when Marisa faced the enormity of her loss.

People said the pain eased with time but Marisa didn't believe it. Half of her had been ripped away, leaving a yawning void that nothing could fill.

The pounding of the falls, like the pulse of a giant animal, melded with the rapid tattoo of her heartbeat. It beckoned her, the way Stefan had time and again. When she closed her eyes she could almost hear the teasing lilt in his voice. *Come on, Rissa. Don't tell me you're scared.*

No, she wasn't scared of anything, except the vast aloneness that engulfed her now Stefan was gone.

Without thought she began climbing towards the tiny ledge beside the fall, taking her time on the treacherously wet rock.

She was almost there when a sound stopped her.

Marisa turned her head and there, just to her right, was

Damaso Pires, the big Brazilian she'd been avoiding since the trek had started. Something about the way he watched her with those knowing dark eyes always unsettled her, as if he saw right through what Stefan had dubbed her 'party princess' persona.

There was something else in Damaso's gaze now. Something stern and compelling that for a moment reminded her of her uncle, the all-time expert in judgement and condemnation. Then, to her amazement, he smiled, the first genuine smile he'd given her.

Marisa grabbed at the cliff as energy arced through her body, leaving her tingling and shaky.

He was a different man with that grin.

Dark and broodingly laconic, he'd always had the presence and looks to draw attention. Marisa had surreptitiously watched the other women simper and show off and blatantly offer themselves to him.

But when he smiled! Heat slammed through her in the wake of a dazzling blast of raw attraction.

His dark hair was plastered to his skull, emphasising the masculine beauty of his bone structure. Tiny streams of water ran from his solid jaw down his strong throat.

It was only then that Marisa realised he wasn't wearing a safety helmet.

It was the sort of thing Stefan would have done in one of his wilder moments. Did that explain the sudden tug of connection she felt?

The Brazilian jerked his head up and away from the falls, his ebony eyebrows rising questioningly.

Following his gesture, Marisa remembered Juan telling them about a lookout beyond the falls and a rough track that curved down from it to the valley floor.

She met those fathomless eyes again. This time their gleam didn't disturb her. It beckoned. Her body zinged with unexpected pleasure, as if recognising an equal.

With a nod she began to clamber up and away from the

sheer plunge of water. He climbed beside her, each movement precise and methodical, till in the end she had to make a conscious effort not to watch him. Weary now, Marisa needed all her concentration for the climb. The spurt of energy that had buoyed her had abated.

She was almost at the top, her vision limited to the next tiny hold, her breath ragged in her ears, when a hand appeared before her. Large, well-kept but callused, and bearing the silvery traces of old scars, it looked like a hand you could rely on.

Arching her neck, Marisa peered up and met liquid dark eyes. Again she felt that jolt of awareness as heat poured through her. Heat that had everything to do with the sizzle in Damaso Pires's gaze as he stood above her on an outcrop of rock.

Marisa hesitated, wondering what it was about this man. He was different from the rest. More…real.

'Take my hand.'

She should be used to that rich accent now. It was a week since she'd arrived in Brazil. But, teamed with Damaso's dark, velvet voice, the sultry seduction of it made something clutch inside.

A quiver rippled through her. She ignored it and made herself reach for his hand, feeling it close hard around her fingers. His strength engulfed her. As she watched, his lips curved in a smile of pure satisfaction.

Awareness pulsed through their joined hands and Marisa knew something like anxiety as his expression sharpened. For a moment he looked almost possessive. Then he was hauling her up, not waiting for her to find the purchase of another foothold.

His display of macho strength shouldn't have made her heart hammer. When she'd been in training she'd known plenty of strong, ultra-fit men.

But not one of them had made her feel as feminine

and desirable as she did now, standing, grubby and out of breath, before this man.

His eyes held hers as he deftly undid her helmet and drew it away. The breeze riffled her damp hair, tugging strands across her face. She knew she looked a mess, but refused to primp. Instead she returned his stare, cataloguing achingly high cheekbones set aslant an arresting face of dark bronze, a long nose with more than a hint of the aquiline, a firm mouth, unsmiling now, and heavy-lidded eyes that looked as if they held untold secrets.

The way he looked at her, so intent, so direct, made her feel like he saw *her*—not the celebrity princess but the woman beneath, lost and alone.

No man had ever looked at her like that.

His gaze dropped to her mouth and her lips tingled. She swallowed hard, unprepared for the sexual need that swamped her as she inhaled his scent—clean, male sweat and something else—soap, perhaps—that reminded her of the sea.

'*Bem vinda, pequenina.* Welcome, little one. I'm glad you decided to join me.'

She stood, looking up at him, her chin tilted, revealing the slender line of her pale throat. Her eyes, the purest azure he'd ever seen, held his, unblinking. And all the while his body tightened, impossibly aroused by the touch and sight of her.

How would she taste?

The question dried his mouth and set his libido spinning.

'Is this the lookout Juan spoke of?' She didn't move away but slipped her hand from his as she turned to admire the view. It was stupendous, the sort of thing people travelled continents to experience. Yet Damaso suspected she used it as an excuse to avoid him.

Too late for that. He'd felt the throb of mutual awareness.

He'd recognised desire in her eyes even as she'd clung like a limpet to the vertical rock.

There would be no more avoiding what was between them. The time for that was past.

'What were you doing, over by the falls?' The words shot out—an accusation he hadn't intended to voice. But the memory of fear was a sharp tang on his tongue. It had sent him swarming up the cliff face without bothering with safety gear.

There'd been something about the way she'd climbed—a determination—as she'd headed for the exposed, most dangerous part of the cliff that had sent a chill scudding down his spine.

What *had* she been up to?

The shadowed, almost dazed look in her eyes when she'd turned to face him on the cliff had shot a premonition of danger through him. Growing up where he had, Damaso had a well-honed instinct for danger in all its forms. He hadn't liked what he'd read in the princess's eyes.

She shrugged. 'Just looking.' Her tone was off-hand, as if she hadn't just risked her life on one of the country's most notoriously treacherous climbs. 'I remembered Juan talking about that boy's dive into the pool.'

Anger stirred at her recklessness. Damaso opened his mouth to berate her then noticed the taut muscles in her neck and her rigid posture. She was like a guard on parade.

Or a princess deflecting impertinent questions?

She had a lot to learn if she thought he'd be so easily dismissed.

He lifted a hand and stroked long, golden strands from her cheek and back over her shoulder.

Her hair was as soft as he'd imagined.

She said nothing, didn't even turn, but he watched with satisfaction as she swallowed.

'The forest seems to go on for ever.' Her voice had a husky quality that hadn't been there before. Damaso smiled.

She was out of danger now and she was here with him. Why probe what she clearly didn't want to talk about?

'It would take days to walk out, and that's if you didn't get lost along the way.' He couldn't resist reaching out to sweep a phantom lock of hair off her cheek. Her skin was hot, flushed with exertion, and so soft he wanted to slide his fingers over all of her, learning her body by touch before testing it with his other senses.

A pulse throbbed at the base of her neck, like a butterfly trapped in a net.

Heat drove down through Damaso's belly as he imagined licking that spot.

Her head jerked around and he was snared by her electric-blue gaze.

'You know the forest well, Senhor Pires?'

She sounded like a courtier at a garden party, her tone light with just the right amount of polite interest. But the cool, society veneer merely emphasised the hot, sexy woman beneath. The fact she was dishevelled, like a woman just risen from her lover's arms, added a piquant spice.

Damaso was burning up just looking at her.

And she knew it. It was there in her eyes.

Awareness sizzled between them.

'No; I'm city bred, Your Highness. But I get out to the wilderness as often as I can.' Damaso always allowed himself one break a year, though he took his vacation checking out one of his far-flung companies. This year it was an upmarket adventure-travel company.

He had a feeling the adventure was just about to start.

'Marisa, please. "Highness" sounds so inflated.' A spark of humour gleamed in her bright eyes. It notched the heat in his belly even higher.

'Marisa, then.' He liked the sound of it on his tongue, feminine and intriguing. 'And I'm Damaso.'

'I don't know South America well, Damaso.' She paused

on his name and a shiver of anticipation raced under his skin. Would she sound so cool and composed when he held her naked beneath him? He didn't know which he'd prefer, that or the sound of her voice husky with pleasure. 'I haven't visited many of the cities.' She reached out and picked a leaf off his open collar. The back of her fingers brushed his neck and his breath stalled.

A tiny smile played at the corner of her mouth. Her eyes told him the lingering touch had been deliberate. Siren!

'My birthplace isn't on anyone's must-see list.' Now *there* was an understatement.

'You surprise me. I hear you're something of a legend in business circles. Surely they'll be putting up a sign saying "Damaso Pires was born here"?'

He plucked a twig from her hair and twirled it between his fingers. No need to tell her no one had any idea where exactly he'd been born, or whether there'd even been a roof for protection.

'Ah, but I wasn't born with a silver spoon in my mouth.'

She blinked, her mouth thinning for an infinitesimal moment, so that he wondered if he'd blundered in some way. Then she shrugged and smiled and he lost his train of thought when she took the twig from his fingers, her hand deliberately caressing his. That light touch drew his skin tight across his bones as lust flared.

'Don't tell anyone,' she smiled from under veiled eyes as if sharing a salacious secret. 'But silver spoons aren't all they're cracked up to be.'

With a quick twist of the wrist he captured her hand in his. Silence throbbed between them, a silence heavy with unspoken promise. Something kindled in her eyes. She returned his hungry look, not resorting to coyness.

'I like the way you face challenges head-on,' he found himself admitting, then frowned. Usually he measured his words carefully. They didn't just shoot out.

'I like the fact you don't care about my social status.'

Her hand shifted in his hold, her thumb stroking his. It pleased him that she didn't pretend disinterest, or lunge at him desperately. The sense of a delicate balance between them added a delicious tension to the moment.

'It's not your title I'm interested in, Marisa.' Her name tasted even better the second time. Damaso leaned forward, eager for the taste of her on his tongue, then stopped himself. This wasn't the place.

'You don't know how glad I am to hear that.' She planted her palm on his shirt and his heart leapt into overdrive. It felt as if she'd branded him.

Tension screwed his body tight. He wanted her *now* and, given the way her fingers splayed possessively on him, her lips parting with her quickened breathing, she felt the same.

He wanted to take her here, hard and fast and triumphantly. Except instinct told him he'd need more than one quick taste to satisfy this craving.

How had he resisted her for a whole week?

'Perhaps you could tell me on the way back down exactly what you *are* interested in, Damaso.'

He snagged her hand in his again and turned her towards the rough track leading away from the cliff. Her fingers linked with his, shooting erotic pleasure through him that felt in some strange way almost innocent. How long since he'd simply held a woman's hand?

Marisa towel-dried her hair while looking out at her private courtyard in the luxurious eco-resort. A bevy of butterflies danced through the lush leaves.

She tried to focus on how she'd capture them on film but all she could think about was Damaso Pires. The feel of his hand enclosing hers as they'd clambered down the track. The wrench of loss when he'd let her go as they'd approached the others. The way his burning gaze had stripped her bare.

No wonder she'd avoided him.

But now she craved him. She, who'd learned to distrust desire!

Yet this was something new. With Damaso Pires she sensed a link, a feeling almost of recognition, that she'd never experienced. It reminded her a little of the very different bond she'd shared with Stefan.

Marisa shook her head. Was grief clouding her thoughts?

Physical exertion, even danger, didn't ease her pain. Since Stefan's death she'd been shrouded in grey nothingness, till Damaso had reached out to her. Could she do it? Give herself to a stranger? Excitement and fear shivered through her. Despite what the world believed, Marisa wasn't the voracious sexpot the press portrayed.

Then she remembered how she'd felt trading words with him, their bodies communicating in subtle hints and responses as ancient as sex itself.

She'd felt happy. Excited. That aching feeling of isolation had fled. She'd felt alive.

A knock sounded on her door, reverberating through her hollow stomach. Second thoughts crowded in, old hurts. Marisa glanced in the mirror. Barefoot, damp hair slicked back from a face devoid of make-up, she looked as far from a princess as you could get.

Did he want the real woman, not the royal? She wavered on the brink of cowardice, of wanting to pretend she hadn't heard him. She'd taken chances on men before and been disappointed. More, she'd been eviscerated by their callous selfishness.

The knock came again and she jumped.

She had to face this.

With Damaso, for the first time in years, she dared risk herself again. That tantalising link between them was so intense, so profound. She *wanted* to trust him. She wanted desperately not to be alone anymore.

Her heart pounded as she opened the door. He filled the space before her, leaning against one raised arm. His eyes looked black and hungry in the early-evening light. Her stomach swooped.

With a single stride he entered the room, closing the door quietly behind him, eyes holding hers.

'Querida.' The word caressed her as his gaze ate her up. If he was disappointed she hadn't dressed up, he didn't show it. If anything his eyes glowed warm with approval. 'You haven't changed your mind?'

'Have you?' She stood straighter.

'How could I?' His smile was lop-sided, the most devastating thing she'd ever seen. Then one large palm cupped her cheek and he stepped close. His head lowered and the world faded away.

CHAPTER TWO

'*MALDIÇÃO!* WHAT YOU do to me.' Damaso's voice rumbled through her bones, his hands gripping tight at her hips as his mouth moved against her ear. Marisa shivered as her hyper-aware nerve endings protested at the sensory overload.

She'd never felt so vulnerable, so *naked*. As if their love-making had stripped her bare of every shield she'd erected between herself and a hostile world.

Yet, strangely that didn't scare her. Not with Damaso.

Marisa clutched his bare back, sleek and damp, heaving slightly as he fought for breath. His chest pushed her down into the wide mattress and she revelled in the hard, hot weight of him, even the feel of his hairy legs imprisoning hers.

All night Damaso had stayed, taking his time to seduce her, not just with his body but with the fierce intensity he'd devoted to pleasing her. He was a generous lover, patient when unexpected nerves had made her momentarily stiff and wooden in his arms. She'd been mortified, sure he'd interpret her body's reaction as rejection. Instead he'd looked into her eyes for an endless moment, then smiled before beginning a leisurely exploration of every erogenous zone on her body.

Marisa shivered and held him tight. Holding him in her arms felt...

'I'm too heavy. Sorry.'

Before she could protest, he rolled over onto his back,

pulling her with him. She clung fast, needing to maintain the skin-to-skin contact she'd become addicted to in the night.

Marisa smiled drowsily. She'd been right: Damaso *was* different. He made her feel like a new woman. And that wasn't merely the exhaustion of a long night's loving speaking.

'Are you all right?' She loved the way his voice rippled like dark, molten chocolate in her veins. She'd never known a man with a more sensuous voice.

'Never better.' She smiled against his damp skin then let her tongue slick along the solid cushion of his muscled chest. He tasted of salt and that indefinable spicy flavour that was simply Damaso.

He sucked in a breath and her smile widened. She could stay here, plastered to him, for ever.

'Witch!'

His big hand was gentle on her shoulder, lifting her away. After lying against the furnace of his powerful body, the pre-dawn air seemed cold against her naked skin. She opened her mouth to protest but he was already swinging his legs out of bed. She lifted a hand to catch him back then let it drop. He'd be back once he'd disposed of the condom. Then they could drowse in each other's arms.

Marisa hooked a pillow to her, trying to make up for the loss of Damaso. She buried her nose in its softness, inhaling his scent, letting her mind drift pleasurably.

They had another week left on the tour. A week to get to know each other in all the ways they'd missed. They'd skipped straight to the potent attraction between them, bypassing the usual stages of acquaintanceship and friendship.

Anticipation shimmied through her. The promise of pleasure to come. Who'd have thought she could feel so good when only yesterday…?

She shook her head, determined to enjoy the tentative optimism filling her after so long in a grey well of grief.

Marisa looked forward to learning all those little things about Damaso—how he liked his coffee, what made him laugh. What he did with his time when he wasn't looking dark and sulkily attractive like some sexy renegade, or running what someone in the group had called South America's largest self-made fortune.

A sound made her turn. There, framed in the doorway, stood Damaso, watching her.

The first fingers of dawn light limned his tall body, throwing his solid chest, taut abdomen and heavy thighs into relief. The smattering of dark hair on his chest narrowed and trickled in a tantalising line down his body. Marisa lay back, looking appreciatively from between slitted eyes. Even now, sated after their loving, he looked formidably well-endowed. As if he was ready to…

'Go to sleep, Marisa. It's been a long night.' The dark enticement of his voice was edged with an undercurrent she couldn't identify.

Shoving the spare pillow aside, she smoothed her arm over the still-warm space beside her.

'When you come back to bed.' She'd sleep better with him here, cradling her as before. It wasn't sex she craved but his company. The rare sense of wellbeing he'd created.

Damaso stood, unmoving, so long anxiety stroked phantom fingers over her nape. Almost, she reached out to drag up the discarded sheet. She hadn't felt embarrassed by her nudity earlier, when he'd looked at her with approval and even something like adoration in his gaze. But this felt different. His stare was impenetrable, that tiny pucker of a frown unexpected.

The silence lengthened and Marisa had to clench her hands rather than scoop up the sheet. She'd never flaunted herself naked but with Damaso it had felt right. Till now.

He prowled across the room with a grace she couldn't

help but appreciate. He stopped at the edge of the bed, drawing in a deep breath. Then he bent abruptly to scoop something off the floor—his discarded jeans. He dragged the faded denim up those long thighs.

Surely he had underwear? she thought foggily, before the implication struck.

Her gaze met his and rebounded from an impenetrable black stare. Gone was the spark of excitement in his gaze, the wolfish hunger that should have scared her yet had made her feel womanly and powerful. Gone was the sizzle of appreciation she'd so enjoyed when they'd sparred verbally.

His eyes held nothing.

'You're leaving.' Her voice was hollow. Or was that her body? Ridiculously, she felt as if someone had scooped out her insides.

'It's morning.' His gaze flicked to the full-length window.

'Barely. It's still hours till we need to be up.' How she spoke so calmly, she didn't know. She wanted to scuttle across the bed and throw herself into his arms, beg for him to stay.

Beg… Marisa had never begged in her life.

Pride had been one of her few allies. After years facing down family disapproval and the wilder accusations of the ravenous press, she'd been stripped of everything but pride. Now she was tempted to throw even that away as desperation clutched at her.

'Exactly. You should get some sleep.'

She blinked, confused at the hint of warmth in his voice, so at odds with his unreadable expression. She felt like she'd waded into knee-deep water and suddenly found herself miles out to sea.

More than ever Marisa wanted to cover herself. Heat crept from her feet to her face as his hooded gaze surveyed her. Was that a flicker of regret in his eyes?

'It's best I go now.'

Marisa bit down a protest. Perhaps he was trying to protect them from gossip, leaving her room before even the staff were up. But since the pair of them had missed dinner last night it was probably too late for that.

'I'll see you at breakfast, then.' She sat up, pinning a bright smile on her face. There would be time enough to spend together in the next week.

'No. That won't be possible.' He finished the buttons on his shirt and strode to the bedside table, reaching for his watch.

'It won't?' She sounded like a parrot! But she couldn't seem to engage her brain.

He paused in the act of wrapping his watch around his sinewy wrist.

'Listen, Marisa. Last night was remarkable. *You* were remarkable. But I never promised you hearts and flowers.'

Indignation stiffened her spine, almost dousing the chill dread in her veins. 'I hardly think expecting to see you at breakfast has anything to do with *hearts and flowers,* as you so quaintly put it.'

Damn him! She leaned down and grabbed the sheet, pulling it up under her arms. At least now she wasn't quite so naked.

'You know what I mean.' The hint of a growl tinged his deep tone and Marisa felt a tiny nub of satisfaction that she'd pierced his monumental self-assurance. For that was what it was—that unblinking stare from eyes as cool and unfeeling as obsidian.

'No, Damaso, I don't know what you mean.' She regarded him with what she hoped looked like unconcern, despite the fact she was crumbling inside.

'I gave no commitment.' As lover-like statements went, this one hit rock bottom.

'I didn't ask for any.' Her voice was tight.

'Of course you didn't.' Suddenly he looked away, intent

on his watch. 'You aren't the type. That's why last night was perfect.'

'The type?' Out of nowhere a chill crept over her bare shoulders.

'The type to cling and pretend a night in bed means a lifetime together.'

His eyes met hers again and she felt the force of desire like a smack in the chest. Even as he rejected her the air sizzled between them. Surely she didn't imagine that? Yet the jut of his jaw told her he was intent on ignoring it.

There she'd been, daydreaming that this might be the start of something special. That, after a lifetime of kissing frogs and finding only warty toads, she might actually have found a man who appreciated her for herself.

She should have known better. Such a man didn't exist.

Marisa's stomach plunged, reopening that vast chasm of emptiness inside.

'So what did it mean to you, Damaso?' She clipped the words out.

'Sorry?'

He looked perplexed, as if no woman had ever confronted him like that. But Damaso was an intelligent man. He knew exactly what she was asking.

'Well, clearly you don't want me expecting a repeat of last night.' Even now she waited, breathless, hoping she was wrong. That he *did* want to spend more time with her, and not just for sex. Marisa wanted it so badly that she discovered she'd curled her hands into hard fists, the nails scoring her skin.

'No.' He paused, his face very still. 'This can't go anywhere. There's no point complicating things further.'

Complicating? Now there was a word. The sort of word men used to denigrate what made them uncomfortable.

'So, out of curiosity…' She kept her voice even with an effort. 'What was last night to you? Did you make a bet with the others that you could get me into bed?'

'Of course not! What sort of man do you think I am?'

Marisa raised her eyebrows, surveying his shocked expression with a dispassionate eye even as hurt carved a channel through her insides. 'I don't know, that's the point.'

She'd vowed never to be burned again. Yet here she was, regretting the impulse that had made her open herself to him.

Marisa had been so sure that this time she'd found a man who at least had no hidden agenda. How many times did she have to learn that particular lesson? Bitterness soured her tongue.

'So it was the princess thing, was it? You'd never done it with a royal?'

He loomed over her, his jaw set.

'Why are you being deliberately insulting?'

And it wasn't insulting, the way he was shoving her aside once he'd had what he wanted, without as much as a 'good morning' or a 'thank you' or even a 'see you later'?

Bile burned in the pit of her stomach and she swallowed hard when it threatened to rise. She wouldn't give him the satisfaction of seeing how he'd hurt her. She'd finally reached out to someone, trusted herself with a man…

Marisa bit her cheek, cutting off that train of thought. She'd been right to hesitate when he'd held out his hand to her on the climb. If only she'd followed her instinct and not touched him.

'I merely want to get it clear in my mind.' She rose and wrapped the sheet around her. She still had to look up at him but at least she wasn't sitting like a supplicant at his feet.

'It was sex, great sex. That's all.' Suddenly there was fire in his eyes and a frisson of angry energy sparked from him. 'Is that what you needed to hear?'

'Thank you.' She inclined her head, wondering how she'd managed to invest simple animal attraction with such significance.

Because she was so needy?

Because she was so alone?

What a pathetic woman she was. Maybe her uncle was right after all.

'Marisa?'

She looked up to find Damaso frowning. This time it was concern she read on his features. He'd even moved closer, his hand half-lifted.

Marisa stiffened. She didn't need anyone's pity, especially this man who'd seen her as perfect for just a night, no strings attached. No doubt, like too many others, he saw her as a woman who wouldn't mind being bedded then shunned.

Her skin crawled and pain stabbed hard between her ribs. It was all she could do not to clutch at her side, doubled up at the force of what she felt.

'Well, if we've finished here, you might as well go.' She looked past him to the bathroom. 'I have a yearning for a long, hot shower.' She wished she could scrub away the hurt that welled as easily as she could wash away the scent of his skin on hers. 'And don't worry; I won't look out for you at breakfast.'

'I won't be here. I'm leaving.'

Marisa blinked and looked away, making a production of gathering up her robe where it had been discarded last night.

So there'd never been a chance for them at all. Damaso had always planned to leave and hadn't had the decency to tell her.

That, as nothing else, clarified exactly what he thought of her. She'd never felt so bruised by a man, so *diminished*. Not since the night Andreas had admitted he'd bet his friends he could get her into bed.

Pain swelled and spread, threatening to poleaxe her where she stood. She had to get away.

Marisa drew herself up and headed for the bathroom.

She paused in the doorway, clutching it for support, and looked over her shoulder.

To her surprise, Damaso hadn't moved. He watched her with a scowl on his face. A scowl that did nothing to reduce the magnetism of his honed features.

He opened his mouth to speak and Marisa knew she couldn't bear to hear any more.

'I wonder if that makes me a notch on your belt or you a notch on mine?' Her voice was a throaty drawl, the best she could manage with her frozen vocal chords.

Then, with a flick of the trailing sheet that only long hours' practice in a ball gown and train could achieve, she swept into the bathroom and locked the door behind her.

'It's a pleasure to have you visit, sir.' The manager smiled as he led the way.

Damaso strode through the lodge, his gaze lingering approvingly on the lofty spaces, the mix of local stone, wood and vast expanses of glass that gave this mountain eyrie an aura of refined, ultra-modern luxury. He'd been right to build it, despite the problems constructing on such a site. Even after a mere six months the place had become a mecca for well-heeled travellers wanting to experience something different.

Beyond the massive windows the vista was stunning as the setting sun turned the jagged Andean peaks and their snowy mantle a glowing peach-gold. Below, even the turquoise surface of the glacier-fed river was gilded in the last rays of light.

'Your suite is this way, sir.' The manager gestured Damaso and his secretary forward.

'I'll find it myself, thanks.' Damaso's eyes remained fixed on the remarkable view.

'If you're sure, sir.' The manager paused. 'Your luggage has been taken ahead.'

Damaso nodded dismissal to both men and headed into

the main lounge. Something about the stillness and the feeling of being up above the bustle of the world drew him. Not surprising, given he'd worked like the devil for the last month, his schedule even more overloaded than usual.

Yet, no matter how frenetic his days or how short his nights, Damaso hadn't found his usual pleasure in managing and building his far-flung empire.

Something niggled at him. A sense of dissatisfaction he hadn't the time or inclination to identify.

He looked around, surprised to find the vast room empty. Turning, he strolled towards a door through which came the hum of voices. The bar was this way. Perhaps he'd have a drink before dinner. He had a full night ahead with his laptop before tomorrow's inspection and meetings.

Laughter greeted him as he stepped across the threshold, halting him mid-stride. Rich laughter, infectious and appealing. It coiled through his belly and wrapped tight around his lungs.

His pulse gave a hard thump then took off.

He knew that laugh.

Damaso's neck prickled as if delicate fingers brushed his nape, trailing languidly and drawing his skin tight with shivering awareness.

Marisa.

There she was, her golden hair spilling around her shoulders, her smile pure invitation to the men crowded close. Her eyes danced as she spoke, as she leaned towards them as if sharing some confidence. Damaso couldn't hear what she said over the thunder of blood pounding in his ears.

But there was nothing wrong with his eyes. They traced the black dress that hugged her sinuous curves. The hemline hovered high above her knees, making the most of the contrast between sparkly black stretch fabric and shapely legs that would make grown men sit up and beg.

He should know. He'd spent hours exploring those legs along with every inch of her delectable body. Everything about her had enthralled him, even the long, curving sweep of her spine had been delicious. *Was* delicious.

A wave of energy surged through him. He found himself stepping forward until his brain clicked into gear. Did he mean to stalk across and rip her away from her slavering fans? What then? Throw her over his shoulder and take her to his room?

A resounding *yes* echoed through his whole being.

That stopped him in his tracks.

There'd been a reason he'd left her so abruptly a month before.

Left? He'd run as fast as he could.

It had nothing to do with business commitments and everything to do with the unprecedented things she'd made him *feel*. Not just desire and satiation, but something far bigger.

He'd got out of her bed with every intention of returning to it then had realised for the first time in his life there was nowhere else he wanted to be.

The idea was utterly foreign and completely unnerving.

That was when he'd decided to order a helicopter back to the city. Not his finest moment. Even with his date-them-then-dump-them reputation, he usually displayed far more finesse in leaving a lover.

Even now part of him regretted leaving her after just one night. What they'd shared had been amazing.

Marisa's gurgle of laughter floated in his ears. Damaso swung round and walked back the way he'd come.

Once was enough with any woman. This…reaction to Princess Marisa of Bengaria was an anomaly. He didn't do relationships. He couldn't. Nothing would ever change that.

He strode up the stairs and along a wide corridor to the owner's suite.

She was nothing to him. Just another party girl. Had she even gone home after the rainforest vacation? Probably not. She was probably whiling away a couple of months in exclusive resorts at her nation's expense while trying out some new lovers along the way.

His teeth ground together and his pace picked up.

There was a tap on the conference-room door before a concerned-looking staff member entered.

'I'm sorry to interrupt.' Her eyes shifted from the manager to Damaso, his secretary and the other senior staff at the large table.

'Yes?' the manager asked.

She shut the door behind her. 'One of the guests has been taken ill on the slopes. They're coming back now.'

'Ill, not an accident?' Damaso heard the note of worry in the manager's voice. Illness was one thing; an accident under the supervision of the lodge's staff was another.

'It sounds like altitude sickness. She only arrived yesterday.'

'She?' Damaso surprised himself by interrupting.

'Yes, sir.' The woman twisted her hands together, turning back to her boss. 'That's why I thought you should know. It's Princess Marisa.'

'You've called a doctor?' Damaso found himself standing, his fists braced on the table.

'Don't worry, there's one on staff,' the manager assured him. 'Only the best for our clients, as you know.'

Of course. That was what set Damaso's hotels apart— attention to detail and the best possible services.

'The doctor will be with her as soon as she arrives,' the manager assured Damaso, nodding dismissal to the staff member, who backed out of the door.

Damaso forced himself to sit but his focus was shot. For the next half hour he struggled to concentrate on profits, projections and the inevitable glitches that arose with any new enterprise. Finally he gave up.

'I have something to attend to,' he said as he stood and excused himself from the meeting. 'You carry on.'

He knew he was behaving inexplicably. Since when did Damaso Pires delegate anything he could do himself? Especially when he'd crossed the continent to take these meetings personally.

Five minutes later he was stalking down a quiet corridor, following a nervous maid.

'This is the princess's suite, sir.' She gestured to the double doors with their intricately carved rock-crystal handles. Tentatively she knocked but there was no answer.

Damaso reached for the door and found it unlocked. 'It's okay,' he murmured. 'I'm a friend of the princess.' Ignoring her doubtful gaze, he stepped inside and closed the door behind him.

'Friend' hardly described his relationship with Marisa. They didn't *have* a relationship. Yet curiously he hadn't been able to concentrate on the business that had brought him here till he checked on her himself.

The sitting room was empty but on the far side another set of double doors was ajar. He heard the murmur of a woman's voice followed by the deeper tones of a man.

'Is it possible you're pregnant?'

CHAPTER THREE

'No!' THE WORD jerked out in shock. 'I'm not pregnant.' Still shivery from nausea, Marisa squinted up at the doctor.

Her? A mother? Why would she bring a child into the world when she couldn't get her own life on track?

She could just imagine her uncle's horror: impulsive, unreliable Marisa who frittered her time away with unsuitable interests rather than knuckling down to the role she was born to. Not that he had faith in her ability to perform that role.

'You're absolutely certain?' The doctor's gaze penetrated and she felt herself blush as she hadn't since she'd been a teen.

She waved one hand airily. 'Technically, I suppose it's possible.' She drew a slow breath, trying to ease her cramped lungs as images she'd fought hard and long to obliterate replayed in her head. 'But it was just one night.'

'One night is all it takes,' the doctor murmured.

Marisa shook her head. 'Not this time. I mean we…he used a condom. Condoms.' The blush in her cheeks burned like fire. Not from admitting she'd been with a man; after all, she was twenty-five.

No, the scorching fire in her face and belly came from the memory of how many condoms they'd gone through—just how insatiable they'd been for each other. Until Damaso had said he wanted nothing more to do with her.

'Condoms aren't a hundred per cent effective, you

know.' The doctor paused. 'You're not using any other contraceptive?'

'No.' Marisa's mouth twisted. All those years on the Pill while she'd been in training and now… Should she have kept taking it?

'Forgive me for asking but how long ago was this night you're talking about?'

'Just over a month ago. A month and a day, to be exact.' Her voice sounded ridiculously husky. She cleared her throat, telling herself to get a grip. Her periods weren't regular—the time lapse meant nothing. 'But I've had no other symptoms. Surely I would have? It has to be altitude sickness. That's what the guide thought.'

Even now the room swooped around her when she moved.

The doctor shrugged. 'It could be. On the other hand, your nausea and tiredness could indicate something else. It's best we rule out the possibility.' He delved into his bag and held something out to her. 'Go on, it won't bite. It's a simple pregnancy test.'

Marisa opened her mouth to argue but she was too wrung out to fight. The sooner she proved him wrong, the sooner he'd give her something to make her feel better.

Reluctantly she took the kit and headed to the bathroom.

Damaso stood unmoving, staring blindly at the sunlight pouring across the richly carpeted floor.

He didn't know what stunned him more—the possibility of Marisa being pregnant, or the fact he'd been her only recent lover.

When he'd left her in the rainforest he'd expected her to find someone else to warm her bed. The way she'd teased those guys in the bar just last night—pouting and showing off that taut, delectable body—he'd been certain she'd ended the night with a man.

If the press was to be believed, she had no scruples about sharing herself around.

Yet she'd been so certain there'd only been him.

That was why Damaso had stayed where he was during the conversation. Eavesdropping wasn't his style, but he was no fool. His wealth made him a target for fortune hunters. It had seemed wiser to wait and hear what she admitted to the doctor in case she tried to bring a paternity suit.

His mouth tightened. He was no woman's easy prey.

But then he recalled the raw shock in her voice. She wasn't playing coy with the doctor—that much was clear. She'd been speaking the truth about the date. If anything there'd been a tremor almost of fear in her voice at the thought of unplanned pregnancy.

A month and a day, she'd said. So precise. Which meant that if she *was* pregnant it was with Damaso's baby.

Shock rooted him to the spot. He was always meticulous about protection. Inconceivable to think it had failed this time.

Even more inconceivable that he should have a child.

Alone almost from birth, and certainly for as long as he could remember, Damaso had turned what could have been weakness into his greatest strength—self-sufficiency. He had no one and needed no one. It had always been that way. He had no plans for that to change.

He plunged his hand through his hair, raking it back from his forehead. He should have had it cut but this last month he'd thrown himself into work with such single-minded focus there'd been no time for fripperies.

A month and a day. His gut churned.

A murmur of voices dragged his attention back to the other room. In two strides he was there, arm stretched out to open the door.

Then his arm fell as the unthinkable happened.

'Ah, this confirms it, Your Highness. You're going to have a baby.'

* * *

Marisa wrapped her arms around herself as she stared out at the remarkable view. The jagged peaks were topped with an icy covering that the setting sun turned to candy pink, soft peach, brilliant gold and every shade in between. Shadows of indigo lengthened like fingers reaching down the mountain towards her, beckoning.

Realisation struck that this was one invitation she couldn't take up. No more climbing for her, no skydiving or white-water rafting if she was pregnant. All the activities she'd used to stave off the grimness of her life were forbidden.

For the hundredth time Marisa slipped her palm over her belly, wonderment filling her at the fact she was carrying another life inside her.

Could the doctor be wrong?

Marisa felt fine now, just a little wobbly and hollow. She didn't *feel* as if she was carrying a baby.

She'd head to the city and have another test. After all, the kit wasn't infallible.

Marisa didn't know whether to hope it was a mistake or hope it wasn't—she was too stunned to know how she felt.

One thing she was sure of, though—she wouldn't be raising any baby of hers within sight of Bengaria's royal palace. She'd protect it as fiercely as any lioness defending her cub.

'Excuse me, ma'am.' Marisa turned to find a smiling maid at the open door from the suite out to the private terrace where she sat. 'I've brought herbal tea and the chef has baked some sesame-water crackers for you.' She lifted a tray and Marisa caught the scent of fresh baking. Her mouth watered. She hadn't eaten since breakfast, worried about bringing on another bout of nausea.

'I didn't order anything.'

'It's with the hotel's compliments, ma'am.' The maid

hesitated a moment then stepped out onto the terrace, putting her laden tray on a small table.

'Thank you. That's very thoughtful.' Marisa eyed the delicate biscuits and felt a smile crack her tense features. The doctor must have organised this.

Leaving the edge of the balcony, she took a seat beside the table. An instant later the maid bustled back, this time with a lightweight rug.

'It's cooling down.' She smiled. 'If you'd like?' She lifted the rug.

Silently Marisa nodded, feeling ridiculously choked as the downy rug woven in traditional local designs was tucked around her legs. How long since anyone had cossetted her? Even Stefan, who'd loved her, had never fussed over her.

She blinked and smiled as the maid poured scented, steaming tea and settled the plate of biscuits closer.

'Is there anything else I can get you, ma'am?'

'Nothing. Thank you.' Her voice sounded scratchy, as if it came from a long distance. 'Please thank the chef for me.'

Alone again, Marisa sipped the delicately flavoured tea and nibbled a cracker. It tasted divine. Or perhaps that was simply because her stomach didn't rebel. She took another bite, crunching avidly.

She needed to make plans. First, a trip to Lima and another pregnancy test. Then… Her mind blanked at the thought of what came next.

She couldn't bear to go back to her villa in Bengaria. The memories of Stefan were too strong and, besides, the villa belonged to the crown. Now Stefan had gone, it belonged to her uncle and she refused to live as his pensioner. He'd demand she reside in the palace where he could keep an eye on her. They'd had that argument before Stefan had been cold in his grave.

Marisa drew the rug close. She'd have to find a new home. She'd put off the decision for too long. But where?

Bengaria was out. Every move she made there was reported and second-guessed. She'd lived in France, the United States and Switzerland as a student. But none were home.

Marisa sipped her tea and bit into another biscuit.

Fear scuttled through her. She knew nothing about being a mother and raising children. Her pregnancy would be turned into a royal circus if she wasn't careful.

Well, she'd just deal with that when and if the time came, and hope she was more successful than in the past.

'Marisa?'

Her head swung round at the sound of a fathoms-deep voice she'd never expected to hear again. Her fingers clenched around delicate bone china as her pulse catapulted.

It really was him, Damaso Pires, filling the doorway to her suite. He looked big and bold, his features drawn in hard, sharp lines that looked like they'd been honed in bronze. Glossy black hair flopped down across his brow and flirted with his collar, but did nothing to soften that remarkable face.

'What are you doing here?' She put the cup down with a clatter, her hand nerveless. 'How did you get in?'

'I knocked but there was no answer.'

Marisa lifted her chin, remembering the way he'd dumped her. 'That usually means the person inside wants privacy.'

'Don't get up.' He stepped onto the terrace, raising his hand, as if to prevent her moving.

She pushed the rug aside and stood, hoping he didn't see her sway before finding her balance. The nausea really had knocked the stuffing out of her.

'I repeat, Senhor Pires, why are you here?' Marisa folded her arms. He might top her by more than a head but she knew how to stand up to encroaching men.

'Senhor Pires?' His brows drew together in a frown that

made her think of some angry Inca god. 'It's a little late for formalities, don't you think?'

'I *know*,' she said, stepping forward, surging anger getting the better of her, 'that I've a right to privacy.'

Her stomach churned horribly as she remembered how he'd made her feel: an inch tall and cheap. She'd have thought she'd be used to it after a lifetime of not measuring up. But this man had wounded her more deeply because she'd been foolhardy enough to believe he was different.

He digested her words in silence, his expression unperturbed.

'Well?' Marisa tapped her foot, furious that her indignation was mixed with an unhealthy dollop of excitement. No matter how annoyed she was, there was no denying Damaso Pires was one fantastic looking man. And as a lover...

'Let me guess. You discovered I was here and thought you'd look me up for old times' sake.' She drew a quick breath that lodged halfway to her lungs. 'I'm afraid I'm not interested in a trip down memory lane. Or in continuing where we left off.'

She had more self-respect than to go back to a man who'd treated her as he had.

She stepped forward. 'Now, if you'll excuse me, I'd like to be alone.'

Her steps petered out when she came up against his impassable form. His spread legs and wide shoulders didn't allow space for her to pass.

Dark eyes bored into hers and something tugged tight in her belly. If only she could put it down to a queasy stomach but to her shame Marisa knew she responded to his overt, male sexuality. A frisson of awareness made her nape tingle and her breasts tighten.

Surely a pregnant woman wouldn't respond so wantonly?

The thought sideswiped her and her gaze flickered from his. Today's news had upended her world, leaving her feeling adrift and frail. What did she know about pregnancy?

'Marisa.' His voice held a tentative edge she didn't remember. 'Are you all right?'

Her head snapped up. 'I will be when I'm allowed the freedom of my own suite, *alone*.'

He stepped back and she moved away into the sitting room, conscious with every cell in her body of him looming nearby. Even his scent invaded her space, till she had to focus on walking past and not stopping to inhale.

She was halfway across the room, heading for the entrance, when he spoke again. 'We need to talk.'

Marisa kept walking. 'As I recall, you made it clear last time I saw you that our…connection was at an end.' Valiantly she kept her voice even, though humiliation at how she'd left herself open to his insulting treatment twisted a searing blade through her insides.

'Are you trying to tell me you thought otherwise?'

Her steps faltered to a halt. If she'd truly been unaffected by his abrupt desertion, she wouldn't be upset at his return, would she? She certainly wouldn't show it. But it was beyond even Marisa's acting powers to pretend insouciance. The best she could manage was haughty distance.

She needed him out of the way so she could concentrate on the news she still had trouble processing. That she was probably pregnant—with *his* child.

Marisa squeezed her eyes shut, trying to gather her strength. She'd face him later if she had too. Now she needed to be alone.

'I didn't think anything, *Damaso*.' She lingered over his name with dripping, saccharine emphasis. 'What we shared is over and done with.'

Her fingers closed around the door handle but, before she could tug it open, one long arm shot over her shoulder. A large hand slammed palm-down onto the door before her, keeping it forcibly closed. The heat of Damaso's body encompassed her, his breath riffling her hair as if he was breathing as hard as she.

'What about the fact you're carrying my child?'

She gasped. *How did he know?*

Marisa stared blankly at the strong, sinewy hand before her: the light sprinkling of dark hairs; the long fingers; the neat, short nails.

She blinked, remembering how that hand had looked on her pale breast, the pleasure it had wrought. How she'd actually hoped, for a few brief hours, she'd found a man who valued her for herself. How betrayed she'd felt.

'Marisa?' His voice was sharp.

She drew a jagged breath into tight lungs and turned, chin automatically lifting as he glowered down at her from his superior height.

The sight of him, looking so lofty and disapproving, stoked fire in her belly. She'd deal with him on *her* terms, when *she* was ready.

'I don't know what you think gives you the right to come here uninvited and throw your weight around. But it's time you left. Otherwise I'll have the management throw you out.'

Damaso stared into blazing azure eyes and felt something thump hard in his belly. Energy vibrated off her in waves. Just meeting her stare sent adrenalin shooting into his bloodstream.

His body tensed, his groin tightening at the challenge she projected.

She tempted him even as her disdainful gaze raked him. But it wasn't only dismissal he read in her taut features. The parted lips, the throbbing pulse, the fleeting shadow in her bright eyes gave her away.

He aroused her. He sensed it as surely as he recognised the symptoms in his own body. He hadn't got her out of his system even now.

Without thinking, he put his hand to her face, cupping her jaw so that a frantic pulse jumped against his skin. His fingers brushed her silk-soft hair.

She felt every bit as good as he remembered. Better than he'd allowed himself to believe. He leaned towards her, lowering his head. Discussion could wait.

Sudden pain, a white-hot flash of agony, streaked up his arm.

Stunned, Damaso saw she'd fastened on to a pressure point in some fancy martial arts manoeuvre. He sucked in a breath, tamping down his instinctive response to over-power her. He'd never learned to fight by any code of rules. Where he'd grown up, violence had been endemic, brutal and often deadly. In seconds he could have her flat on her back in surrender. He forced himself to relax, ignoring the lancing pain.

'I'm calling the management.' She breathed heavily, as if it was she, not he, in agony.

'I *am* the management, *pequenina*.'

'Sorry?' Her fierce expression eased into owlish disbelief.

'I own the resort.' Damaso tried to move his fingers but another dart of pain shot through him. 'You can let me go,' he said through gritted teeth. 'I promise not to touch you.'

'You own it?' Her grip loosened and he tugged his hand free, flexing it as pins and needles spread up his arm. For an amateur, her self-defence skills were impressive.

'I do. It was my team of architects who designed it. My builders who constructed it.'

'The staff report to you?' Her tone was sharp. 'That explains a lot.' Her mouth tightened. 'I don't see why the doctor should run to you with news of my health, even if you employ him. What about patient confidentiality?' She didn't raise her voice but the way she bit out the words, as if chipping off shards of glacial ice, spoke volumes.

Damaso shook his head. 'He didn't breathe a word.'

At her frown he explained, 'I was here, in the suite, when he confirmed your test results.'

She stared up at him, her eyes bright as lasers, and just

as cutting. Damaso felt his cheeks redden, almost as if he blushed under her accusing stare.

It was impossible, of course. Embarrassment was a luxury denied those who'd survived by scavenging off others' refuse. Nothing fazed him, not even the shocked accusation in her glare. He didn't care what others thought.

Yet he looked away first.

'I'd heard you were ill and came to see how you were.'

'How very considerate.' Her hands moved to her hips, pulling the fabric of her designer T-shirt taut over those delectable breasts. Belatedly, Damaso tore his gaze away, only to find himself staring at her flat stomach. She cradled his baby there. The shock of it dried his throat. He wanted to slip his hand beneath the drawstring of her loose trousers and press his palm to the softness of her belly.

The snap of fingers in front of his face startled him.

'Being the owner of this place doesn't give you the right to pry into my private life.'

'It was unintentional. I was coming to see you.'

'That's no excuse for spying on what is my affair.'

'Hardly spying, Marisa.' Her flashing eyes told him she disagreed. 'And this *affair* affects both of us.'

Colour streaked her cheekbones, making her look ridiculously young and vulnerable.

He softened his voice. 'We need to talk.'

She shook her head, her bright hair slipping like spun gold across her dark shirt. With quick grace she turned and crossed the room to the vast windows framing the view of the Andes. She stood rigid, as if his presence pained her.

'A month and a day, remember, Marisa? This is as much my business as yours.'

She didn't move, not so much as a muscle. Her unnatural stillness disturbed him.

'When were you going to tell me?'

Still she said nothing. Damaso's skin tightened till it felt like hundreds of ants crawled over him.

'Or weren't you going to? Were you planning to get rid of it quietly with no one the wiser?'

Damaso grimaced at the pungent sourness filling his mouth. Had she decided to get rid of his child?

His child!

He'd been stunned by the news he was to be a father. It had taken hours to come to grips with the fact he'd have a child—blood of his blood, flesh of his flesh.

For the first time in his life, he'd have family.

The idea astounded him, scared him. He, who'd never expected to have a family of his own. Yet to his amazement part of him welcomed the idea.

He didn't know exactly how he expected this to play out. But one thing was absolutely certain: no child of his would be abandoned as he'd been.

No child of his would grow up alone or neglected.

It would know its father.

It would be cared for.

He, Damaso Pires, would make sure of that personally. The intensity of his determination was stronger than anything he'd known.

He must have moved for he found himself behind Marisa. Her hair stirred with each breath he exhaled. His fingers flexed, as if to reach for her hips and pull her to him, or shake her into speech.

'Say something!' Damaso wasn't used to being ignored, especially by women he'd known intimately. Especially when something as profoundly important as this lay between them.

'What do you want me to say?' When she turned, her eyes were wide and over-bright. 'No, I hadn't planned an abortion? No, I hadn't decided when I'd tell you, if at all? I haven't had time even to get my head around the idea of being pregnant.'

She jabbed a finger into his sternum. 'I don't see this being as much your business as mine.' Her finger stabbed again. '*If* I'm pregnant, I'll be the one carrying this baby. *I'll* be the one whose body and life and future will change irrevocably. Not you.'

Her finger wobbled against his chest; her whole hand was shaking, Damaso realised. He wrapped his hand around hers but she tugged loose from his hold and backed away as if his touch contaminated her.

Too late for that, my fine lady.

Marisa watched his harsh mouth curve in a smile that could only be described as feral. He looked dangerous and unpredictable, his eyes a black gleam that made her want to step back again. Instead she planted her feet.

How had he turned the tables, so his intrusion on her privacy had become a litany of accusations against *her?* Enough was enough. She was tired of being bullied and judged.

'Obviously you've had time to jump to all sorts of conclusions about this pregnancy, if there is one.' She fixed him with a stony gaze.

'You deny it?' He scowled.

'I reserve judgement until I've got a second opinion.' She braced her hands on her hips, refusing to cower before his harsh expression. 'But obviously you've gone beyond that stage.'

'I have.' His gaze dropped to her stomach and she felt a hot stirring inside as if he'd touched her there. Abruptly, his dark eyes locked on hers again. 'There's only one sensible option.'

'Really?'

'Of course.' His brooding features tightened, a determined light in his eyes. 'We'll marry.'

CHAPTER FOUR

MARISA COULDN'T PREVENT the ripple of laughter that slipped from her mouth.

'Marry?' She shook her head. Astonishment punctured the bubble of tension cramping her chest. 'You've got to be kidding. I don't even know you.'

His downturned mouth and furrowed brow told her he didn't appreciate her levity. Or maybe he didn't like the panicked edge that see-sawed through her laughter.

Marisa didn't like it either. She sounded, and felt, too close to the edge.

'You knew me well enough for us to create a baby together.' His deep voice held a bite that eradicated the last of her semi-hysterical laughter. It brought her back to earth with a thump.

'That's not knowing. That's sex.'

He shrugged, lifting those broad shoulders she'd clung to through their night together. She'd dug her nails into his flesh as ecstasy had consumed her. She'd never wanted to let him go and had snuggled against his solid shoulder through the night.

Until he'd made it clear he wanted nothing more to do with her.

'You've changed your tune.' Did he hear the echo of hurt in her tone? Marisa was beyond caring; she just knew she had to scotch this insanity.

'That was before there was a child, *princesa*.'

She stiffened. 'There still may not be one. I won't be sure till I've had another test. It could have been a false positive.'

Damaso tilted his head, as if examining a curious specimen. 'The idea of a child is so horrible to you?'

'No!' Marisa's hand slipped to her stomach then, realising what she'd done, she dropped her arm to her side. 'I just need to be sure.'

He nodded. 'Of course. And when we are sure, we'll marry.'

Marisa blinked. Why did talking to Damaso Pires feel like trying to make headway against a granite boulder?

'This is the twenty-first century. People don't have to marry to have children.'

He crossed his arms, accentuating the solid muscle of his torso beneath the pristine business shirt, reinforcing his formidable authority. Wearing casual trekking gear, he'd been stunning, but dressed for business he added a whole new cachet to the 'tall, dark, handsome' label.

If only she didn't respond at that visceral, utterly feminine level. She couldn't afford to be distracted by such rampant masculinity.

'We're not talking about *people*. We're talking about us and our child.'

Our child. The words resonated inside Marisa, making her shiver. Making the possibility of pregnancy abruptly real.

She put out a hand and grabbed the back of a nearby settee as the world swam.

Suddenly he was there before her, his hand firm on her elbow. 'You need to sit.'

It was on the tip of her tongue to say she needed to be alone but she felt wobbly. Perhaps she should rest—she didn't want to do anything that might endanger her baby.

And just like that she made the transition from protest to acceptance.

Not only acceptance but something stronger—something like anticipation.

Which showed how foolish she was. This situation had no built-in happy ending.

Marisa let Damaso guide her to a seat. The pregnancy no longer felt like a possibility, to be disproved with a second test. It felt *real*. Or maybe that was because of the way Damaso held her—gently, yet as if nothing could break his hold.

She lowered her eyes, facing the thought of motherhood alone. Learning to be a good mother when she had no idea what that was. The only things she'd ever been good at were sports and creating scandal.

Marisa bit down a groan, picturing the furore in the Bengarian royal court, the ultimatums and machinations to put the best spin on this. The condemnation, not just from the palace, but from the press.

In the past she'd pretended not to feel pain as the palace and the media had dealt her wound after wound, slashing at her as if she wasn't a flesh-and-blood woman who bled at their ferocious attacks.

'I'll get the doctor.' Damaso crouched before her, his long fingers still encircling her arm.

'I don't need a doctor.' She needed to get a grip. Wallowing in self-pity wasn't like her and she couldn't afford to begin now. More than ever she had to find a way forward, not just for herself, but for her child.

'You need someone to care for you.'

'And you're appointing yourself my protector?' She couldn't keep the jeering note from her voice.

For the first time since he'd shouldered his way into her suite, he looked discomfited. Eventually he spoke.

'The baby is my responsibility.' He spoke so solemnly, her skin prickled.

'Sorry to disillusion you but I don't need a protector. I look after myself.' She'd learned independence at six, when her mother had died. Now she only had vague memories of warm hugs and wide smiles, of bedtime stories and an exquisite, never-to-be-repeated certainty she was precious.

'Reading the press reports about your activities, I can see how well you've done that.'

Marisa's chin shot up, her furious gaze locking with his. 'You shouldn't believe everything you read in the press.'

Except everyone did, and eventually Marisa had given up trying to explain. Instead she'd been spurred to a reckless disregard for convention and, at times, her own safety.

That stopped now. If there was a baby…

'So I should give you the benefit of the doubt?' He leaned closer and her breath snared in her lungs. Something happened to her breathing when Damaso got near.

'I don't care what you think of me.' In the past that had worked for her. But with Damaso things were suddenly more complicated.

'I can see that. But I also see you're unwell. This news has come as a shock.'

'You're not shocked? Just how many kids do you have littered around the place?' Marisa strove for insouciance but didn't quite achieve it. Absurdly, the thought of him with a string of other women made her stomach cramp.

'None.'

Ah. Maybe that explained his reaction.

'Let me propose an interim arrangement.' He sat back on his haunches, giving her space.

It was a clever move, she realised, as her racing pulse slowed.

'Yes?'

'You want a second pregnancy test. Let me take you to the city and arrange a medical examination. Then, if the results are positive, we talk about the future.' He spread his hands in a gesture of openness.

Yet the glint in his dark eyes hinted things weren't so simple.

But what did she have to lose? He only proposed what she'd already decided. And, as owner of the lodge, he could get her out of here quickly, without waiting for a scheduled flight.

'No strings?'

'No strings.'

Doubt warred with caution and a craven desire to let someone else worry about the details for once. If he tried to trample her, he'd learn he was messing with the wrong woman.

'Agreed.' She put out her hand, using the business gesture to reinforce that this was a deal, not a favour. A tiny bubble of triumph rose at his surprised look.

But, when his hand encompassed hers, engulfing her in its hard warmth, her smile faded.

Marisa twisted in her seat as the helicopter's rotors slowed. Damaso saw anger shimmer in her eyes as she glared at him. 'You said we'd go to the city.'

'São Paolo is inland, not too far away.'

'You lied to me.' Her mouth set in a mutinous pout that made him want to pull her close and kiss those soft, pink lips till all she could do was sigh his name.

Damaso stared, grappling with both his urgent response and surprise at her vehemence.

'I said I'd take you to have your pregnancy confirmed.' Even now, after a day to absorb the news, he felt a pooling of emotion at the thought of the baby they'd created.

'In a city. That's what we agreed. That's why I agreed to come to Brazil with you. I thought when we transferred from the plane we were going into São Paolo.'

'I've organised for a doctor to visit you here, in my private residence.'

Marisa's gaze roved the view beyond his shoulder, past the ultra-modern mansion looking over a pristine beach and aquamarine water to the tangle of lush forest rising up the slope beyond. 'It's secluded,' he murmured. 'I own the whole island.'

'You think that's a recommendation? I have no interest in your *private* estate.' Her jaw clenched, as if she read what he'd tried to suppress—the physical hunger that still plagued him.

From the moment he'd seen Marisa, he'd wanted her. One night in her bed had only sharpened his appetite, and not just for her lithe body. He wanted to possess all of her: her quicksilver energy; her laughter; her earthy, generous sexuality and that feeling she shared some rare, exquisite gift with him. Even arguing with her was more stimulating than sealing a multi-billion-dollar deal.

This craving disturbed him. Usually he found it easy to move on from a woman. But then, he'd never had one carry his child before. That must be why he couldn't get her out of his head.

'Lots of women would give their eye teeth to be here.'

She looked at him with a supercilious coolness that made him feel, for the first time in years, inferior. 'Not me.'

The smack to his lungs, the hot blast of blood to his face, shocked him to the core.

He was Damaso Pires, self-made, successful, sought after. He bowed to no one, gave way to no one. He'd banished the scars of childhood with the most convincing cure of all: success. Inferiority was a word he'd excised from his personal lexicon years before.

'You're not impressed, *princesa?*'

Her eyes widened a fraction. Because he'd called her 'princess', or because he'd growled the words between gritted teeth?

'It's not about being impressed.' She spoke coolly. 'I simply don't like being lied to.'

Damaso drew a slow breath and unclicked his seat belt. 'It wasn't a lie. I often commute to the city from here.' He put up his hand before she could interrupt. 'Besides, I thought you'd appreciate the privacy of my estate, rather than go to a clinic or have an obstetrician visit you in a city hotel.' He stared into her sparking blue eyes. 'Less chance of the paparazzi getting hold of the story, since my staff are completely discreet.'

He watched her absorb that: the quick swallow, the rushed breath through pinched nostrils.

Ah, not so superior now. Obviously she didn't want news of her condition made public.

'Thank you.' Her quick change of tone surprised him. 'That's thoughtful of you. I hadn't considered that.' She fumbled at her seatbelt so long, he looked down and saw her hands were unsteady. He wanted to reach out and do it for her but her closed expression warned him off.

At last the seatbelt clicked open and she pushed it away. 'But don't ever lie to me again. I don't appreciate being lured here under false pretences.'

It was on the tip of Damaso's tongue to say he wasn't interested in luring her anywhere. But that was exactly what he'd done, because it suited his purposes. Much as it went against the grain to admit it, she had a point.

'Very well. In future you will be consulted.'

Her perfect dark-gold eyebrows arched. 'In future,' she corrected in a voice of silk-covered steel, 'I *decide*.'

In one easy movement she swung her legs out of the door, held open by one of his staff, and strode away from the tarmac of the landing pad without waiting to see if he followed.

She walked like a princess, head up, shoulders straight, with a firm gait that wasn't a stride but somehow conveyed her absolute confidence that the world would rearrange itself to fit her expectations.

He told himself she was spoiled and wilful. Instead, he found himself admiring her. He wasn't used to having his arrangements questioned.

Her thanks for his thoughtfulness had surprised him.

Her firm insistence on making her own decisions was something he understood.

He watched the cream linen of her trousers tighten around her shapely backside with each step, watched the way her hair, a thick curtain of gold, swung between her narrow shoulder-blades.

In future he'd remember to take the time to convince Princess Marisa to agree to his decisions before he put them into action.

Damaso's mouth curved in a rare smile as he got down from the chopper and followed her. Persuading Marisa presented all sorts of interesting possibilities.

Marisa strode from the house mere moments after the doctor had left her. Not just any doctor, but the region's best obstetrician, apparently, and a woman to boot. Damaso had thought of everything.

No doubt he was closeted with the doctor, receiving confirmation of the pregnancy.

Marisa's step quickened till she reached the soft, white sand of the beach where she tugged off her sandals.

She wanted to sprint down the beach till her lungs burned, swim out into the impossibly clear depths of the bay till she was totally isolated from the luxury mansion full of staff. Climb the rocky headland that jutted at the far end of the beach.

Anything to feel free again, if only briefly.

Marisa sighed. She needed to be more cautious now she was pregnant. She could sprint, of course, but the security guard trailing her would think she was under threat. If she explained, he'd feel obliged to race up the beach beside her, destroying her enjoyment.

Reluctantly she looked back and there he was: a bulky figure trying, ineffectually, to blend into the foliage just above the beach.

Even in Bengaria she'd had more freedom!

Marisa waded into the warm shallows till she was up to her calves, letting the tiny waves lap against her legs. She breathed deep, trying to feel at one with the gentle surge and wane of the water, focusing on slowing her pulse.

It was years since she'd practised the techniques she'd used to prepare herself for a gymnastics competition. If ever she'd needed to feel grounded, it was now.

She was going to be a mother.

Joy, mingled with fear, spilled through her veins. Despite the circumstances, she couldn't regret the child she carried. Did she have what it took to raise it and care for it the way it deserved?

She had no one to turn to, no one to trust, but Damaso: a stranger who saw this baby as a responsibility.

Fleetingly, Marisa thought of the others who'd claim a say in her child's future.

Her relatives. She shivered and wrapped her arms around her torso. No matter what it took, she'd keep her child safe from them.

The advisors of the Bengarian Court. No, they'd simply follow her uncle's lead.

Her friends. Marisa bit her lip. She'd given up seeking real friends long ago—after the few she'd had were ostracised by the palace for being too uncultured and common for her to mix with.

Which left her alone.

Her smile was crooked as she gazed towards the mainland. She'd always been alone, even when Stefan had been alive. There was only so much he'd been able to do to support her. He'd had his own troubles. She'd been lucky—as a mere princess, she was window dressing, for she'd never inherit the crown. Poor Stefan, as crown prince, had borne the brunt of everyone's expectations from birth.

'Marisa.'

She swung around to see Damaso at the water's edge. In lightweight trousers and a loose white shirt, sleeves rolled up past his elbows, he looked too sexy for her peace of mind.

Her heart crashed against her ribs and her lungs tightened, squeezing the air from her body till she felt breathless and light-headed. Her skin tingled as his dark gaze slid over her. She was burning up, a pulse throbbing between her legs.

'We need to talk.'

'You don't waste time, do you?' She crossed her arms. 'What do you mean?'

'You've come straight from the doctor, haven't you?' He'd said they'd find out if she was pregnant then they'd talk about the future. 'Can't you give me some breathing space?'

She hadn't meant to say it aloud but she felt hemmed in by news of the pregnancy, by the security guard, by the fact she'd have to tell her uncle. Above all, by this man, who for reasons she didn't understand made her *feel,* right to her core.

'I'm not going to hurt you.'

Marisa sucked in a breath. 'I'm not afraid of you, Damaso.' How dared he even think it? She, who'd never turned from a physical challenge in her life.

'No?' She supposed that tightening of his mouth at one corner was supposed to be a smile. She didn't see anything funny about the situation.

'Absolutely not.' Facing down a sexy Brazilian with an ego the size of Rio's Sugarloaf Mountain was nothing compared with what she'd dealt with before.

Yet she didn't move to join him. Instead he waded out to meet her, the water covering first his bare feet then soaking his trousers. Marisa's mouth dried as if she hadn't tasted water in a week.

He stopped a breath away, his scent mingling with the salt tang of the water.

'How do you feel?'

'Fine.' It was true. She'd been sick again this morning but tea and dry toast in bed and a slow start to the day had made the nausea easier to handle.

'Good. We need to talk.' His intent scrutiny made the hairs stand up on the back of her neck. Some sixth sense told her he wasn't here to continue an argument about marrying for the baby's sake.

'What is it?' She'd received bad news before and, attuned after Stefan's recent death, she knew Damaso would rather not break this news. 'Is it the baby?' Her voice was a hoarse whisper. 'Did the doctor tell you something she didn't tell me?'

He took her elbow as she lunged towards him, her heart pounding frantically. 'It's not the baby. Nothing like that.'

Instinctively Marisa planted her hand on his chest, needing his support. She felt the steady thud of his heart beneath her palm and managed to draw a calming breath. She pushed down a moment's terror that there'd been something the doctor hadn't shared.

'What, then? Tell me!'

His mouth thinned to a grim line. 'It's the press. There's been a report that you're pregnant.'

'Already?' Her head swung towards the multi-level residence commanding the half-moon bay.

'It wasn't one of my staff. No one here would dream of going to the press with a story about a guest of mine.'

'How can you be sure?' Something passed across his face that Marisa couldn't fathom. 'For the right sort of money…'

He shook his head. 'My people wouldn't betray me.'

Fleetingly, Marisa wondered what bond could possibly be so strong between a billionaire and his paid staff.

'It was someone from the hotel in Peru. One of the kitchen staff. They overheard my request for something to settle your morning sickness.'

'*Your* request?' Marisa dragged her hand back from his

chest as if scalded. She'd thought the doctor had ordered tea and crackers for her.

The thought of Damaso leaving her room and heading to the kitchens to make a personal request on her behalf made her still. It didn't fit with the way he'd treated her. But, now she considered it, since learning of her pregnancy he'd been intent on looking after her.

She'd been too annoyed at his high-handed actions to acknowledge it, possibly because his way of helping was to try taking control.

'It was a new staff member. Now an ex-staff member. They won't work in any of my enterprises again.' The steely note in his voice made Marisa feel almost sorry for whoever had thought to profit from gossiping to the press.

'I thought I'd have a little more time before it became public.' She tried for nonchalance, though an undercurrent of nerves made her body tense. Once the news was out...

'It's an unconfirmed rumour. Nothing they can prove.'

'I suppose I've weathered worse.'

Memories rose of being pilloried at just fifteen. Someone on the gymnastics squad had leaked the fact that Marisa was on the Pill and it had been splashed across the press, along with photos of her partying.

No one had been interested in the fact she'd been prescribed the medication to help deal with periods so painful they'd interfered with her training, or that the parties were strictly chaperoned. Everything had been twisted. Innocent glances in photos turned into lascivious stares, smiles into wanton invitations. They'd portrayed her as a little slut, precocious, uncontrollable and without morals.

Once typecast by the paparazzi, there'd been no way to turn the tide of popular opinion.

The palace had been ineffectual. It was only years later she'd begun to suspect the palace had left her to fend for herself—a brutal lesson in dancing to her uncle's tune or else. Eventually, after years fighting the tide, Marisa had given up and begun to take perverse pleasure in living down to expectations.

She breathed deep and stepped back, registering anew the gentle swish of water against her legs.

'At least I don't have to worry about the press here.' She pasted on a smile. 'Thank you, Damaso. It seems you were right. If I'd stayed in a hotel, I'd be under siege.'

Was it her imagination or did his gaze warm a fraction? 'In the circumstances, I'd prefer not to have been right.'

It was tempting to bask in the fragile sensation of being looked after. But she couldn't afford to get used to it.

They walked side by side up the beach, scooping up their discarded shoes and turning towards the house.

They'd just stepped onto the cropped emerald turf when a white-coated servant appeared and spoke to Damaso in swift Portuguese.

'What is it?' Marisa sensed the instant change in him.

'A message for you. You had a phone call and they're calling back in fifteen minutes.'

'Who was it?' But already Marisa felt her stomach plunge like a rock off a precipice. She knew exactly who it had been.

His words confirmed her fears. 'The King of Bengaria.'

CHAPTER FIVE

DAMASO PACED THE shaded loggia, the tray of coffee and his laptop forgotten. Through the full-length glass he had a perfect view of Marisa.

He'd begun to wish he hadn't given her privacy to take her call. Not when instinct urged him to march in and rip the phone out of her hand.

That, by itself, gave him pause.

He didn't interfere in the lives of others. He was never interested enough to do so. But, watching Marisa stand to attention beside the desk in his study, Damaso knew an inexplicable urge to break the habit of a lifetime.

What was the King saying? As far as he could see, she hadn't had the chance to say much. Yet her body spoke volumes. Her spine was ramrod-stiff and she paced with military precision, like a soldier on parade. Her mouth was a flat line and her shoulders inched high towards her ears.

She wore the figure-hugging white capri pants and yellow crop top from the beach. There she'd looked like a sexy embodiment of the summer sun—bright and vibrant. Now, with her pinched features, she seemed like another woman.

To hell with it. He strode towards the glass doors that separated them.

Then he stopped, for now Marisa was talking.

This close he heard her voice, though not the words. She spoke crisply, with definite emphasis. Her chin lifted and she looked every inch the pure-bred aristocrat: haughty and regal.

She paused, as if listening, then spoke sharply, her arm slicing the air in a violent sweep. She turned and marched across the room, her toned body taut and controlled, ripe with pride and determination.

Damaso stared, unable to believe the visceral stab of desire that hit him as he watched her lay down the law. A woman in control—that had never been his fantasy. Always he was the hunter, the master, the one who set the rules.

Was that what had made their night together so cataclysmically memorable? The sense of two matched people coming together as equals, neither in control?

If that was so, why this unfamiliar urge to protect her? It had to be because of the baby. Since he'd learned of her pregnancy she'd become the centre of his thoughts—a rival even to his business empire, which had given him purpose and identity all his adult life.

Damaso breathed hard, aware he was on unfamiliar ground.

It took him a few moments to realise she'd ended the call. Now she stood, shoulders slumped, hands braced wide on the desk. As he watched, her head bowed in a move that spoke of a bone-deep weariness.

Something stirred in Damaso's belly. That tickle of concern he'd first felt the morning he'd left her in the jungle. When, despite her anger and her hauteur, he'd sensed something out of kilter in her queenly dismissal of him.

'Marisa?' He was through the door before he had time to reconsider.

Instantly she straightened. If he hadn't been looking, he'd never have seen the strain etching her face before she smoothed it.

'Yes?'

Damaso stared, confronted by a cool, self-contained princess, the hint of a polite smile curving her soft lips.

Only the glitter of strong emotion in her eyes, now darkened to midnight sapphire, belied that regal poise.

'What did he want?'

Her delicate eyebrows arched high, as if surprised at his temerity in questioning her. That cut no ice with Damaso.

Silently he waited. Eventually her gaze skittered from his. She shrugged. 'King Cyrill wasn't pleased when his public relations advisors told him there were rumours I was pregnant.'

'They were quick off the mark!'

Her mouth tightened. 'They're always careful to keep tabs on me.' Did he imagine an emphasis on 'me'?

'And what did you say? Did you confirm the pregnancy?' Damaso wished he knew more about the Bengarian monarchy. He'd had no interest in the small European kingdom till someone on the trek had pointed Marisa out as the infamous party princess he'd vaguely heard about. How close were she and the King? Obviously their conversation had taxed Marisa's strength, despite her show of unconcern.

She half-turned and stroked a finger idly along the gleaming surface of his desk. 'It's none of his business.' Defiance edged her tone. 'But then I realised there was nothing to be gained by waiting. I'd have to face the flak sooner or later.'

'Flak? Because you're not married?' He knew next to nothing about royals—except that their lives seemed steeped in tradition.

She laughed, the sound so bitter he wondered if it hurt. 'Not married. Not in a relationship. Not seeing a man vetted and approved by the palace. Not doing what a Bengarian princess is supposed to do. Take your pick.'

Damaso stepped closer, drawn by the pain in her voice. 'What is it you're supposed to be doing?'

Marisa's head lifted, her chin angling, as if facing an opponent.

'Being respectably and sedately courted by a suitable prince, or at least a titled courtier. Keeping out of the press, except in carefully staged set pieces arranged by the palace. Not causing a scandal, particularly now.'

'Now? Why now?' Why hadn't he taken time to find out more about Marisa's European homeland?

Because his focus was and always had been on building his business. That was what he lived for. What made him who he was.

Marisa straightened, but once again refused to meet his gaze. 'I'd like to say it's because the country is still in mourning for Stefan. But it's because Cyrill doesn't want any scandal in the lead up to his coronation.'

At Damaso's enquiring look, she explained. 'Cyrill is my uncle, my father's younger brother. My father was king and after my father died Cyrill was Regent of Bengaria for eleven years, till Stefan came of age at twenty-one.' She sucked in a breath and for a moment he thought she'd finished speaking. 'Stefan was my twin brother and King of Bengaria. He died in a motorboat accident two months ago.'

Two months ago? Damaso frowned, searching her face. Her brother had been barely cold in his grave when Damaso had met Marisa. She hadn't acted like a woman grieving the loss of a loved one.

Yet what did he know of grief or loss? He'd never had so much as a best friend, let alone family.

'You don't like your uncle?'

Marisa turned startled eyes on him, then laughed again, the sound short and sharp. 'I can't stand him.' She paused. 'He was our guardian after our father died and to all intents and purposes King.' Her voice held a sour note that told far more about their relationship than her words. 'Even when Stefan was crowned, Cyrill was there in the background, trying to manipulate opinion whenever Stefan dared to instigate change.'

'But now you're free of him.'

Marisa turned to stare out across the lawns to the sandy crescent of Damaso's private beach. It looked so peaceful, so perfect. But the sight did nothing to calm her. Not after Cyrill's threats.

The last day and a half, she'd been in a state of shock. And now this… Once more her uncle threatened to turn her life inside out.

'It's not that simple.' Foolishly, she'd thought it was. With Stefan gone, Marisa had no interest in Bengarian politics. She just hadn't counted on the fact that Bengaria wasn't ready to wash its hands of her. A fact her uncle had been at pains to point out.

'Marisa? What is it?' Damaso's voice deepened and she forced herself to look up, only to find herself pinioned by his questioning gaze. Between Damaso and her uncle, she had no chance of peace! What she needed was time to sort herself out, away from domineering men. Even if one of them made her question her need for solitude.

'Are you going to tell me or will I ring your uncle?'

Shock warred with laughter at the idea of anyone calling Cyrill on the spur of the moment. Who would win? Her uncle, with his smug self-importance and devious ways, or Damaso with his my-way-or-the-highway approach?

'He wouldn't talk to you.'

'No one is that inaccessible, Marisa.' Damaso crossed his arms, one slashing dark eyebrow lifting in enquiry. He didn't bluster but there was such innate determination in his stance, his expression, she had no doubt her uncle would come off the worse in a contest of wills. 'Why aren't you free of him?'

With a sigh, she sank into a nearby armchair. 'Because he holds the purse strings. As simple as that.' And, fool that she was, she hadn't seen it coming. How could she not have thought of it earlier?

Because she'd been wiped out by grief, grimly battling to face each new day after Stefan's death and not to wear her pain publicly. She'd actually thought she could break her ties with the palace. How naïve, especially after experiencing her uncle's Machiavellian ways first-hand.

Every penny she had was now sequestered by royal command. How was she going to find herself a home and provide for her child when everything she owned no longer belonged to her? Marisa bit her cheek hard as she felt her mouth tremble.

She'd thought she was adrift and rudderless without Stefan, but now...

'He's threatened to stop your allowance?' Damaso's tone was casual.

'Yes, he's stopping my *allowance,* as you call it—the money invested for me by my parents.' She drew a deep breath. 'He's also threatening to freeze my assets, including my personal bank account.'

Fire kindled in Damaso's eyes. 'By what right?'

'By right of the sovereign. In Bengaria, that means everything. He has control over all members of his extended family if he chooses to use it.' She sank back in her seat, weary beyond reckoning. It was a power even her strict father wouldn't have invoked. 'It's legal. Just not ethical.'

That was Cyrill all over. Anything to get his own way.

Who'd have thought his plans would still include her after the breach between them? She shuddered, wondering if he really wanted her back in Bengaria, or whether this was an elaborate tactic to make her suffer for repudiating him.

Damaso sank down before her, his gaze capturing hers. 'You'll want for nothing now you're with me.'

He meant it. It was there in his steady stare.

'Except I'm not *with* you! I haven't agreed to marry you.' Her heart hammered high in her throat as she read his implacable expression.

He didn't say anything. He didn't need to. This was a

man used to giving orders and having them obeyed. Right now he wanted her.

Correction: *he wanted her baby.*

Chilled to the marrow, Marisa crossed her arms, shielding her child.

Damaso and Cyrill both wanted to control her for their own ends. Both wanted her child—Damaso for reasons she didn't fully understand, Cyrill because her baby had royal blood, making it a potential pawn in his elaborate schemes to extend the power of the crown.

'So, go out and get a job. Support yourself.' Impatience edged Damaso's tone. Marisa had heard it before from people who didn't know her but believed all they read in the press.

About to hide her feelings behind the usual show of casual disdain, something stopped her.

Damaso's good opinion shouldn't matter. He'd already shown how little he thought of her. Yet she paused. She was tired of being judged and found wanting.

'You think I haven't tried?' At the surprise in his eyes, she turned away, hunching her shoulder against his disbelief. 'Who'd take me seriously, especially when the press start hounding me, pestering my employer and other staff? Making bets on how long I'll stick it out?'

She shuddered, remembering how her naïve optimism had been shattered again and again. Failure had bred failure. Her reputation hung like an albatross around her neck: dilettante; party girl; frivolous, unable to stick to anything. How many times had she tried to do something worthwhile, only to have the opportunity snatched away?

Last time the press had camped outside the special school where she'd volunteered until both staff and children had become unsettled and nervous. Finally the director had asked her not to come any more.

'I've tried. Don't think I haven't.' Marisa heard the shaky echo of defeat in her voice. It scared her. All she had left was her independence. She'd fought so long for that and she had to be strong now.

Instantly she was on her feet, needing to move, to think.

But Damaso was before her, his large hand wrapping around her wrist before she could take a step.

He looked down into her pale face, her wide eyes, shadowed now instead of bright, and felt the tiniest tremor ripple under her skin. Slowly she lifted her chin as if distancing herself from him. Was it an unconscious gesture, that superior set of the head, or a practised move designed to scare off plebeians such as himself?

Yet, holding her slender wrist, it struck him that behind the air of well-bred hauteur lurked a world of pain.

Damaso was an expert at reading people. It was a skill he'd cultivated and exploited even as a child, gauging which adults would respond to a skinny kid's wide-eyed hungry look with an offer of food and which with a swift kick. But in all his years his understanding had rarely turned to empathy.

Yet, what other explanation could there be for this protectiveness? This need to wrap his arms around her and hold her close?

There were violet smudges under her fine eyes and she couldn't quite disguise the way her lips trembled. She did a magnificent job of hiding it but once more he recognised a vulnerability about Princess Marisa of Bengaria that went far deeper than the mere loss of funds.

His hand gentled on her arm.

'Whatever he does, he can't touch you here.'

It was meant for reassurance, but he felt her stiffen.

'But I haven't said I'd stay.'

Sharp heat twisted in Damaso's belly. He refused to countenance a future where his child grew up without him.

His child.

The words were like a beam of light, illuminating a hollow in the dark void of his soul he'd never known till now.

He'd never thought to belong to anyone. Yet he knew with deep gut instinct that he had to be part of his baby's life. His child would have a father, a family, such as he'd never known. His child would never be alone and frightened. It would never want for anything.

Damaso's hand tightened around Marisa's.

He wasn't the sort to step back from what he wanted. He'd never have survived the slums if he hadn't learned early to take life by the throat and hang on tight.

But there was more than one way to get what he wanted. He was fast learning Marisa wasn't the two-dimensional party girl the world thought she was. He'd seen hints of it from the first. Her revelations about her uncle and her distress when Damaso had snapped that she should get a job had shattered that image.

'Let me go, Damaso. You're hurting me.'

Yet she stood stock still, too proud to fight his hold. Unexpectedly, his chest squeezed at her defiant posture. Holding her as he did, he felt her tremble.

'Am I?' He slid his fingers down to wrap around hers and lifted her hand, inhaling the tang of her skin's scent. Slowly he lowered his head and pressed his lips to the inside of her wrist. Instantly her pulse flickered hard and fast. He kissed her again and heard her swift intake of breath.

'Damaso. Let go of me.' Her voice had a distinct wobble. It reminded him of her broken cry of ecstasy the first time she'd climaxed beneath him. Heat saturated his skin as his libido shifted gear, rousing in an instant.

'What if I don't want to?' Her fingers twitched in his hold as he kissed her again.

Damaso didn't look up. Instead he held her hand and laved the centre of her palm, feeling her tiny shudder of reaction and its echo in the tightening of his groin.

It was a warning that the seducer could also be the seduced. But Damaso had no doubt who was in control. He'd keep Marisa here by whatever means worked—by force, if necessary—but far better to convince her she wanted to remain exactly where she was.

'*I* want you to stay.'

'Really?'

He tugged her hand and she stumbled a half-step closer. Damaso took advantage of her momentum to wrap his other arm around her and draw her close. Slowly, with a thoroughness designed to break the strongest will, he pressed his lips to her wrist again, then higher, planting firm kisses along Marisa's forearm. When he got to her elbow she jerked in his hold, her breath a soft gasp.

Instantly the heat drenching his skin stabbed deep into his belly, igniting a fire that spread to his groin.

He wanted her.

Just like that, he wanted her again. Not only the baby—but Marisa, lithe and sexy, in his bed.

From her elbow he took his time tracing a path up her soft flesh till he reached her bare shoulder. He felt her choppy breathing flutter over his throat, the gentle softening of her body in his hold, and triumph filled him.

She'd stay, and on his terms.

Damaso nuzzled the pulse point at the base of her neck and she arched back, giving him unfettered access.

His groin was rock-hard as he gathered her in and kissed his way up her neck to the corner of her mouth.

Desperate hunger rose. Despite the carnal intimacies they'd shared, he'd yet to taste her lips. She'd always distracted him with her body, her caresses. He intended to remedy that.

He turned his head to take her mouth but she wrenched away. Taken by surprise, he wasn't quick enough to catch her back. She broke free and stood, breathing heavily, one palm pressed to her chest as if fearing her heart might catapult free.

Damaso was about to reach for her when his vision

cleared and he read her expression: confusion, desire and fear, all etched starkly on features drawn too tight.

An iron fist crushed his chest, forcing the air from his lungs.

She looked so weary. Yet she drew herself up, as if to repel a hostile takeover. Her chin angled proudly in that familiar tilt, but her face was flushed, and one hand twisted the edge of her top.

Damaso could seduce her. He'd felt her tremble on the brink of surrender. But at what cost?

For the first time in his life, Damaso pulled back from the edge of victory. Not because he didn't want her but because Marisa wasn't ready.

He breathed deep, stunned at the decision he'd made without thinking—putting her needs before his.

Somehow he managed a smile. He watched her eyes widen.

'I have a proposal, Marisa.'

Instantly she stiffened.

'Stay here while we get to know each other. Relax and recuperate till the morning sickness passes. Take the time to rest and don't worry about your uncle. He can't reach you here.' He swept an arm towards the windows. 'Swim, eat, sleep and take all the time you need. Then later we'll talk. In the meantime treat this as a private resort.'

'*Your* private resort.'

He nodded, barely stifling impatience. 'I'll be here. It's my home.' He neglected to mention his apartment in the city and the other residences scattered around the globe. He had no intention of leaving Marisa. How could he seduce her into staying permanently if he wasn't here?

Eyes bright as lasers sized him up and he had the unexpected sensation Marisa knew exactly what he intended. His hands clenched as she surveyed him. Patience wasn't his strong suit.

Finally, she spoke. 'I have one condition. There'll be no

coercion.' Her eyes flashed. 'As your guest, I expect you to respect my privacy. When I want to leave, you won't try to prevent me. I'm here of my own free will. I refuse to have my movements curtailed.'

Damaso inclined his head, wondering how long it would take to convince her it wasn't privacy she craved.

CHAPTER SIX

A SHADOW BLOTTED the sun and Marisa opened her eyes, squinting up from the sun lounger.

'You'll burn if you stay there any longer.' Damaso's voice turned the warning into a seductive samba of delicious sound. That deep, liquid, ultra-masculine voice, the lilt of his accent, sent her nerves into overdrive.

Immediately her drowsy comfort vanished as her heart took up a wild percussion rhythm. Even after weeks on his island she wasn't immune to the sheer sensual appeal of the man. And she'd tried. How she'd tried!

Her mouth dried as she saw he'd stripped off his shirt, his skin dark-gold in the afternoon sun. The board shorts he wore rode low over his hips, drawing the eye to the sculpted perfection of taut muscle.

A whorl of sensation twisted between her legs, making her shift uneasily.

'I put sunscreen on just a while ago.' Her voice sounded reedy, and no wonder. She'd never met a man as physically compelling as Damaso. Despite her efforts to blot their night together from her memory, she remembered exactly how it had felt, pressed up against that glorious body, embraced by those powerful arms.

She'd never thought she'd regret the end of her morning sickness, but after mere weeks it had waned and without its distraction Marisa found herself conscious of Damaso at a deep physical level that disturbed her.

'Here.' Damaso held up a tube of sunscreen, squirting some onto his palm. 'Let me protect you.'

'No!' Why did his words make her think of another sort of protection altogether? One that had already failed?

Heat scored Marisa's cheeks as she reached out and took the tube from him. 'Thanks, but I'll do it myself.' She did *not* need Damaso's hands on her.

Their time on his island had only escalated her awareness of him. He hadn't touched her, but the intensity in his dark eyes whenever they rested on her was proof he hadn't forgotten their night together either. And, despite the way her thoughts chased round in her head as she tried to plot a future for herself and her baby, Marisa found herself too drawn to this almost-stranger.

The last thing she needed was to give up her independence and allow another man power over her. She would rely only on herself now her baby was on its way. She was determined to protect her child from the negative influences she'd experienced, overbearing men included.

At least Damaso hadn't crowded her during these last weeks. Unlike her uncle, whose constant phone and email messages unsettled her.

Marisa slapped the cream on her arms, across her cleavage and down to her midriff and legs.

Still Damaso stood, unmoving. She felt him watching every slide of her palm and felt heat build deep inside. It was as if he was the one touching her flesh, making her nerves tingle in response to his heavy-lidded stare.

'What about your back?'

For answer, Marisa shrugged into a light linen turquoise shirt.

Was that a smile tugging his mouth at the corner?

'You're a very independent woman, Marisa.'

'What's wrong with that?' In her uncle's book, 'independent' had been synonymous with 'troublesome'.

'Absolutely nothing. I admire independence. It can make the difference between life and death.'

Marisa opened her mouth to ask what he meant when he dropped to his knees beside her, hemming her in. They hadn't been this close, close enough for his body to warm hers, for weeks.

Instantly, sexual awareness hummed through her body and effervesced in her bloodstream. The shocking intensity of it dried her automatic protest.

'You missed a bit,' he murmured, bending close.

Then he was touching her, but not in the long, sensuous strokes she'd expected. Instead his brow furrowed with concentration as he painted sun cream across her nose in gentle dabs, as if she were a child.

She didn't feel in the least childlike.

Damaso's eyelashes were long and lustrous, framing deep-set eyes dark as bitter chocolate. The late sun burnished his face and Marisa's breath hissed between her teeth at the force of the longing that pooled deep inside.

For she wanted him. She wanted his touch, his body, and above all his tenderness, with an urgency that appalled her.

Oh yes, he could be tender when it suited him. But she hadn't forgotten how he'd dismissed her after their night together, when she'd begun to wonder if she'd finally found someone who might value her.

Marisa sat back, jerking from his touch.

Never had she craved a man like this. Was it pregnancy hormones, playing havoc with her senses?

He surveyed her steadily, as if she wore her thoughts on her face. But surely he had no idea what she was thinking? She'd learned to hide her thoughts years ago.

Slowly Damaso lifted his hand but this time he swiped the remaining sun cream across his chest in a wide, glistening arc. Marisa swallowed and told herself to look away. But her fascination with his body hadn't abated. How could it, when in the late afternoon light he looked like some gilded deity, an embodiment of raw masculine potency?

'What's that scar?'

If he noticed the wobble in her voice, he didn't show it. Instead he looked down at the neat line that curved at the edge of his ribs.

'A nick from a knife.' His tone was matter-of-fact, just like his shrug.

Marisa tried not to cringe at the idea of a knife slicing that taut, golden flesh.

'And that one?' She'd noticed it the night they'd spent together: a puckered mark near his hip bone that had made her wince even though it was silvered with age.

'Why the curiosity?'

'Why not?' It was better than dwelling on how he made her feel. With him so close, she couldn't get up and move away, not without revealing how he unsettled her. It was a matter of pride that she kept that to herself.

The gleam in his eyes made her wonder if he knew she was looking for distraction. But he didn't look superior, or amused. Instead, he met her regard steadily.

'You want me to marry you but I don't know anything about you,' she prompted.

It was the first time marriage had been mentioned since she'd arrived, as if by common consent they'd agreed to avoid the matter. Marisa wondered if she'd opened a can of worms by mentioning it again.

Would he try to force her hand now she'd brought it up? That was her uncle's tactic—bulldozing through other people's wishes to get what he wanted.

Damaso crossed his arms over his chest, as if contemplating her question. The movement tautened each bunching muscle, highlighting the power in his torso.

Marisa kept her eyes on his face, refusing to be distracted.

'It was another knife.'

'Not the same one?' She frowned.

'No.'

So much for explanation. This was like drawing blood from a stone. 'You got yourself into trouble a lot when you were young?'

Damaso shook his head. 'I got myself *out* of it. There's a difference.'

At her puzzled look, he shrugged and Marisa swallowed quickly. Did he realise how tempted she was to reach out and explore the planes and curves of his naked torso?

Of course he knew. He watched her like a hawk, seeking signs of vulnerability.

'I'm a survivor, Marisa. That's why I'm still here—because I did what it took to look after myself. I never started a fight, but I ended plenty.'

There was no bravado in his words. They were plain, unadorned by vanity.

The realisation sent a trickle of horror down her spine. She'd had her troubles but none had involved fighting for survival against a knife attack.

'It sounds like life was tough.'

Something flickered in his eyes. Something she hadn't seen before. Then he inclined his head a fraction. 'You could say that.'

Abruptly he moved, rising in a single, powerful surge. He leaned down, reaching to help her up, but Marisa looked away, pretending she hadn't seen the gesture.

She'd never been a coward but inviting Damaso's touch was asking for trouble. She stood unaided then turned back to him, putting a pace between them as she did so. Nevertheless, her skin tingled from being so close.

'What about you? What's the scar at the back of your neck?'

Marisa's head jerked up. He couldn't see the scar now; it was covered by her single thick plait. Which meant he'd noted and remembered it from the night they'd spent together. Heat fizzed from her toes to her breasts as their gazes locked. Damaso had spent his time that night learning her body with a thoroughness that had undone her time and again.

'A fall off the beam.'

'The beam?' One eyebrow arched.

'In gymnastics we sometimes perform on a beam, elevated off the ground. This—' her hand went automatically to the spot on her nape just below her hairline '—was an accident when I was learning.'

'You're a gymnast?' He looked at her as if he'd never seen her before.

'Was. Not any more.' Bitterness welled on her tongue. 'I'm too old now to be a top-notch competitor.' But that wasn't why she was no longer involved in the sport she'd adored, why she wasn't even coaching it. She'd come to terms with that years before, so the sudden burst of regret took her by surprise.

Could pregnancy make you maudlin?

Despite her physical wellbeing after these weeks of rest and privacy from prying eyes, Marisa was unable to settle. Her emotions were too close to the surface. Perhaps all those years repressing them were finally catching up with her.

'I think I'll stretch my legs.' She turned and wasn't surprised when Damaso fell into step beside her, shortening his stride to fit hers.

In silence they walked along the soft sand of the beach. Surprisingly, despite the tug of awareness drawing her belly tight, Marisa felt almost comfortable in his company. If only she could forget about Damaso as a lover.

They'd reached the end of the beach when the thoughts she'd been bottling up demanded release.

'Why, Damaso?' She swung round to find him watching. 'Why do you want marriage?' Though he hadn't raised the idea recently, it still pressed down on her. 'Lots of parents don't marry.'

'Yours were married.'

'That's no recommendation.' She didn't bother to hide her bitterness.

'They weren't happy?'

She shrugged and bent to pick up a shell, pearly-pink and delicate on her palm.

'No, they weren't.' She paused, then sighed. Why not tell him? Then maybe he'd understand her reluctance to marry. 'It was an arranged marriage, made for dynastic reasons. My mother was beautiful, gentle, well-born—and rich, of course.' Her mouth twisted. Bengaria's royal family always looked for ways to shore up its wealth. 'My father wasn't a warm man.' She bit her lip. 'They weren't well-matched.' At least, not from what she remembered and the stories she'd heard. Her mother had died so long ago, she only had a few precious memories of her.

'That doesn't mean all marriages are doomed to failure.'

'So, were your parents happy together?' If he'd grown up in a close-knit, loving family, that might explain why he insisted on marriage.

Damaso watched her in silence so long, she felt tension knot between her shoulder blades.

'I doubt it.'

'You don't know?'

'I don't remember my parents.'

'You're an orphan?'

'No need to sound so shocked. I've had a long time to get used it.' His smile was perfunctory, not reaching his eyes.

'Then why marriage? Why not—?'

'Because I *will* be part of my son's life. Or my daughter's. I'm not interested in child support by proxy. My child will have *me* to support them.' His face was tight and implacable.

Marisa shivered. The way he spoke, all their child needed

was *him*. Where was she in his grand scheme? She intended to be there to protect her baby, come what may.

'You don't trust me to be a fit mother, is that it?' Pain bruised her chest as she thought of the scandal that dogged her. These past weeks had opened up emotional wounds she'd thought long buried. 'You're judging me on what you've read in the press.'

Sure, she'd done her share of partying, but the reality wasn't anything like the media's lurid reports. Her notoriety had gained a life of its own, with kiss-and-tell stories by men she'd never even met.

Damaso shook his head. 'I'm not judging you, Marisa. I'm simply saying I won't settle for a long-distance relationship with my own flesh and blood.' She heard the echo of something like yearning in his deep voice.

Was that it? Did he *want* their child, rather than just feel responsible for it? The idea held a powerful appeal. Already she knew she'd do whatever was needed to ensure her baby's well-being. Marisa blinked up at his stern face, looking for signs of softness.

If only she could read him. It was rare that she sensed the man behind his steely reserve. She saw only what he allowed.

How could she trust a man she didn't know?

'What sort of man would I be to walk away from our child and leave all the responsibility on your shoulders?'

He had no idea how much she wanted support now. But responsibility without caring was a dangerous combination. That was how Cyrill had been with her and Stefan and it had poisoned their lives. She had to protect her baby.

'Doesn't our child have a right to both parents?' His eyes searched hers. She felt the force of his stare right to her toes. 'Doesn't it deserve all the security we can give it?'

'Yes, but—'

'There are no buts, Marisa.' Suddenly his hands were on her shoulders, drawing her close enough to feel the ripple of energy radiating from him. 'I refuse to abandon my child to make its own way in the world. I want to keep it safe, nurture it, care for it and protect it from all danger. I want it never to feel alone. Is that a crime?'

Suddenly, it was as if the rigid blankness of a mask had been ripped aside, revealing a man who, far from being cold and remote, was racked by strong feeling. A man whose hands shook with the force of stark emotion she saw in eyes that glittered almost black.

Is that what had happened to him? Had there been no one to protect and care for him?

Marisa thought of the knife wounds. His previous iron-hard composure. His talk of independence as the difference between life and death.

Horror and pity welled. What had this man survived? How long had he been alone as a child?

But she knew better than to ask. Damaso Pires was many things but an open book wasn't one of them. He'd revealed what he had grudgingly, presumably to convince her to accept him.

'Of course it's not a crime.' Her voice held a husky edge as her see-sawing emotions overcame her diffidence. She lifted a hand and planted it on his chest—to comfort and reassure, she told herself. Yet the sharp thud of his heart beneath her palm told her it would take more than that to calm him. She tried not to react to the erotic pleasure of hot, male flesh and crisp chest hair against her palm.

'So you agree.' Triumph blazed in his face. 'Marriage is the only option.'

'I didn't say that.' Marisa backed away, or tried to. His hold on her shoulders stopped her. Those hard fingers flexed and drew her closer, till her hand on his bare torso was all that separated them. His heat encompassed her; the subtle tang of his skin invaded her nostrils, making her recall the salt taste of him the night they'd been lovers. She quivered as a blast of longing rocked her.

'I could persuade you.' His voice dropped to a deep timbre that brushed like raw silk across her skin. His hands softened, smoothing her shoulders and back in a caress that spoke of easy expertise. Marisa bit her lip as her body arched greedily under his touch.

He bent his head, his mouth brushing her hair, his breath hot on her forehead. 'You've kept your distance since we came here, and I've let you pretend, but we both feel the connection. You can't deny it. It's there every time you look at me, every time I look at you. It hasn't gone away.'

His marauding hands swept the curve of her spine and out to her hips. He dragged her close and her breath stopped when she felt his arousal hard against her belly.

She closed her eyes, willing her trembling body to move away. His hold was firm but not unbreakable. She could escape. If she wanted to.

Instead she pressed closer, rising on her toes, bringing them into more intimate contact.

Damaso's breath hissed and Marisa might have felt triumph if she hadn't been swamped by hunger.

He was right. She'd tried to ignore it but this was why she'd been restless. Not just her pregnancy and the quandary over her future. Those were problems for later, eclipsed by the immediacy of her desire for Damaso.

Seeing him daily but keeping her distance had been an exercise in futility. What control she'd clung to now shattered in response to his potent charisma.

Her neck bowed back as he dropped his head and kissed her throat.

'You'd like me to persuade you, wouldn't you? It will be a pleasure for us both. A pleasure we've denied too long.' His mouth, hot and sensual, moved up her neck, kisses becoming tiny, erotic nips that tightened her skin and puckered her nipples. Her hands slid across the planes of his chest, raking slick skin and coarse hair.

Then his hand slid round her hip, delving unerringly in

one quick, sure motion to her feminine core. His fingers pressed hard against the fabric of her bikini bottom, making a pulse thud hard and quick between her legs.

Her breath snagged again and a wisp of sanity invaded her clouded mind. It would be so easy to give in. But something about the knowing ease of his action evoked a memory: Andreas, with his practised seduction technique that she'd been too naïve to recognise. Andreas, who'd used her for his own ends.

Damaso's mouth dipped from her ear to the sensitive point at the corner of her jaw, sending every nerve into tingling ecstasy. Marisa felt him smile knowingly against her skin.

He knew precisely how to seduce her.

One desperate shove and a backward step and she was free, her chest heaving, her legs wobbling as if she'd run for her life. Shock hit her that she'd actually broken away. Her body screamed with loss now he wasn't touching her.

Marisa watched unguarded emotion flit across Damaso's features: shock, anger and desire. Determination.

Her heart sank. If he touched her again, she'd be lost; even knowing his every move was carefully orchestrated to make her putty in his hands.

It wasn't his seduction she fought but herself. Her face flamed.

He moved towards her and she shrank away.

Instantly he stopped.

In the silence all she heard was the thunder of blood in her ears and his ragged breathing.

'Don't.' Her voice was choked and thick. She swallowed hard. Her gaze dipped to the reddened streaks on his heaving chest. Her nails had scored him.

Marisa's scalp tightened as she saw that reminder of her unbridled response. It was one thing to give in to lust when they'd come together as equals. It was another to let herself be coaxed by a man ruthlessly assessing her weakness to achieve his own agenda.

'Please.' She gasped as the word slipped out, but her pride was already in tatters. Her vision glazed and she wanted to hide her face, ashamed at how easily she'd responded.

Forcing her eyes up, she met his slitted gaze. Marisa drew a shuddering breath. 'If you have any respect for me at all, if you want any possibility of a future together, don't *ever* do that again. Not unless you mean it.'

CHAPTER SEVEN

'DAMASO! IT'S BEEN an age.' The once familiar, sultry voice made him turn. It had been months since Adriana had shared his bed but, looking into her exquisite, model-perfect face, it felt like far longer.

Once he'd been eager to accept the invitation in her sherry-gold eyes. Now he looked and felt nothing, not even an echo of past satisfaction.

She was stunning, from her glossy fall of black hair to her ripe curves poured into a flame-coloured dress that looked like liquid fire in the mood lighting. Even the memory of her enthusiasm for pleasing him did nothing to ignite his interest.

'Adriana.' He inclined his head. 'How are you?'

'All the better for seeing you.' Her smile was a siren's, her hand on his jacket proprietorial.

Annoyance tracked a finger down his spine and he shifted, watching her frown as her hand dropped.

'You're not happy to see me?' Her lips were a seductive scarlet pout.

'It's always a pleasure.' Or it had been, until she'd started hinting about staying in his city penthouse and asking about his movements. Possessive women were guaranteed to dampen his libido.

'But not enough to call me.' Damaso opened his mouth to terminate the encounter but she spoke again, pressing close. 'Forgive me, Damaso. I didn't mean that.'

'There's nothing to forgive.' Yet he didn't respond to the blatant offer in her gaze or the way her body melted against his. He stood straighter. She was beautiful, but…

'I see you have a new friend.' Her voice dipped on the word. 'Aren't you going to introduce me?'

He turned to see Marisa threading her way through the throng. Her gold hair was piled elegantly high, adding inches to her small frame. Or maybe it was the way she held herself. The frothy skirt of her scant, sapphire-blue dress swung jauntily above her knees as she walked, drawing covetous glances.

She looked right at home among Brazil's elite as they celebrated. Marisa was chic, gorgeous and effervescent, thriving on the attention of so many besotted men.

She stopped to exchange a laughing comment with a debonair man in exquisitely tailored formal clothes. A man who obviously cared about looking good at Fashion Week's premier event. He might have been a model with that chiselled jaw shadowed with designer stubble.

The stranger reached out and touched Marisa lightly on the hand.

Damaso felt heat ignite deep inside, sparks shooting through his bloodstream. His fingers tightened on his glass as Marisa smiled at the man now blocking her path.

'Although it seems she's otherwise occupied.' Adriana's voice filtered through the fog of pulsing sound in his ears. 'Your princess appears to know a lot of people.'

Across the room she drew yet another slavering admirer into the conversation. She positively sparkled at the epicentre of male attention.

Damaso slammed his glass onto a nearby table, his fingers flexing.

Marisa was *his*. She mightn't admit it yet but she soon would. He could have forced her to do so just days ago on the island. But that haunted look, her desperate dignity when she'd pleaded to be left alone, had stopped him.

Crazy, when he knew she wanted him.

Now the sight of another man, other *men*, fawning over her made him want to smash his fist into one of them. All because of a woman!

'Damaso? Are you okay?' Adriana touched his hand. 'You're burning up! Are you unwell?'

He wrenched his gaze away to focus on Adriana. She looked worried. Perhaps because it was the first time she or anyone had seen him lose his cool.

He'd brought Marisa to the city to keep her occupied while he worked through what had happened that day on the beach. The feelings Marisa provoked scared Damaso as nothing had since he'd been fifteen and he'd taken on the pair of knife-wielding thugs who'd ruled his squalid neighbourhood.

No other woman got to him the way she did.

His jaw tensed and seconds later he was looming over Marisa's admirers. Conversation faltered and they melted away.

'Damaso.' The husky way Marisa said his name, the way her eyes darkened as she looked up at him, made him want to hoist her over his shoulder and forget any pretensions at being civilised. 'I'm glad you're here.'

'Are you? You seemed to be enjoying yourself.' His jaw clenched.

She shrugged, her smile dying as she read his face. What did she see there? Anger? Possessiveness?

Marisa turned away but he wrapped his fingers around her chin, tipping it so he could read her expression. Long lashes veiled her eyes but her lips trembled. The animation bled from her face and he read weariness there, the hint of shadows beneath her make-up.

'Marisa?' Something swooped in his chest. 'What's wrong? I thought you were enjoying yourself.'

If anything was guaranteed to satisfy the party-girl princess, it was this, one of São Paolo's most chic, most exclusive parties. The guest list was a who's who of beautiful people and the music was an enticing pulse-beat of good times.

'It's…nice. I'm just tired.'

'Tired?' The woman who thrived on celebrations? 'I thought you loved this sort of thing.'

'Sometimes.' Marisa's smile was perfunctory. Damaso stared at the taut line of her bare shoulders. Stunned, he realised she was anything but happy.

She broke his hold and turned away, lifting an outrageously decorated cocktail to her lips.

His hand shot out, grasping her wrist. 'Alcohol isn't good for the baby. Especially the potent cocktails they serve here.'

Marisa's mouth flattened. The hairs at his nape rose as her eyes narrowed to needle sharpness.

'You don't think much of me, do you? Here.' She shoved the fruit-laden cocktail towards him so hard it sloshed over the edges, dripping onto her wrist and down her dress. She paid no heed. 'Go on, taste it.'

Dimly he was aware of the buzz of conversation, the curious stares.

'Go on!' Her lips twisted derisively. 'Or are you afraid it's too strong for you?'

Her eyes blazed as she pushed the neon-tinted straw to his lips. Reluctantly he sucked and swallowed.

'Fruit juice!'

'Amazing, isn't it? Imagine me drinking anything but alcohol, when all the world knows I only quaff champagne.'

Abruptly she let go of the glass and he grabbed it before it fell and shattered. Cold, sticky juice dribbled down his hand.

'I didn't have so much as a sip of wine the whole time I was on your precious island.' Her voice was an acerbic hiss as she leaned close. 'Yet you assume I can't control myself as soon as I hit a party.'

A smile curved Marisa's lips but her eyes were flat. 'I see my reputation precedes me.' She drew in a breath that pushed her breasts high and her shoulders back. 'What else did you think—that I'd be off having sex with some man in a dark corner while you chatted with your friends?' She paused, her eyes widening. 'Or, let me guess, with a couple of men? Is that why you looked like some Neanderthal, stomping over here?'

Damaso stared. The whispered vitriol was so at odds with the smile on her delicate features. Anyone watching would think she was playing up to him rather than tearing strips off him.

It hit him with the force of a bomb exploding that Marisa was an expert at projecting an image. Suddenly his certainties rocked on their foundations.

How real had her enjoyment been when she'd laughed with those guys? Had she been putting on a front?

'I came because I wanted to be with you.'

'I'm sure you did.' Her saccharine tone told him she didn't believe a word. 'You had to tear yourself away from your girlfriend. I assume she *is* a girlfriend?'

Damaso stiffened. 'This isn't the place.' He explained his private life to no one, especially to a woman who somehow managed to make him feel in the wrong. It wasn't a familiar sensation and he didn't like it.

'Of course she is.' Abruptly Marisa dropped her gaze. 'Well, far be it from me to play gooseberry. No doubt I'll see you tomorrow.' She turned away. 'Goodnight, Damaso.'

Her arm was supple and cool beneath his palm as he wrapped his hand around it.

Her eyebrows arched in a fine show of hauteur, as if he defiled her with his touch. She looked as she had the day in the jungle when she'd dismissed him so disdainfully. It irked now as it had then.

He didn't give a damn how superior she acted. He wasn't releasing her.

'Where do you think you're going?'

'Back to your city apartment. Where else?'

She looked like an ice maiden, ready to freeze any male foolish enough to approach.

As if that would stop him! She could pretend all she liked but he knew better.

'Good.' Damaso said. 'I'm ready to leave.'

He tucked her hand through his arm and strode out, oblivious to the curious crowd parting before them.

The short helicopter ride to his penthouse was completed in silence. Marisa sat with her face turned, as if admiring the diamond-bright net of city lights below, her profile calm and aristocratically elegant.

She ignored him, as if he was far beneath her attention. Anger sizzled. He wasn't the ragged kid he'd once been, looking in on society from the outside. He was Damaso Pires. Powerful, secure, in command of his world.

Yet he'd watched those men eat her up with their eyes and rage had consumed him. Rage and jealousy.

The realisation hit him with full force.

He didn't do jealousy.

Damaso shook his head.

He did now.

Is that why he'd been so tactless? He had a reputation for sophistication but tonight he'd felt out of control, trapped in a skin that didn't fit.

The chopper landed and soon they were alone in his apartment.

If he'd thought she'd shy from confrontation, he was wrong. Marisa swung around, hands on hips, before he'd done more than turn on a single lamp. In her glittering stilettos, with sapphires at her throat and her short, couture dress swinging around her delectable legs, she looked like any man's dream made flesh.

But it was her eyes that drew him. Despite their flash of fury, he saw shadows there.

He'd done that.

'I'm sorry.' He'd never said that to any woman. Even now he couldn't quite believe he'd spoken the words. 'I overreacted.'

'You can say that again.' Absurdly her combative attitude made him want to haul her close and comfort her. In the past, he'd have walked away from a woman who wasn't totally compliant. But Marisa hooked him in ways he didn't understand.

'I didn't think you'd been drinking or having sex.' Damaso paused. He could have phrased that better.

'And I'm supposed to be impressed by that?'

'No.' He ploughed a hand through his hair, frustrated that for the first time the words hadn't come out right. Usually persuading a woman was easy.

'I'm tired, Damaso. This can wait.' She turned away.

'No!' He lowered his voice. 'It can't. On the island, we got on well.'

'And?'

'And I want to understand you, Marisa.' It was true. For the first time in his life, he wanted to know a woman.

What did that mean?

'I want you to trust me.' That was better. Women loved talk of trust and emotions.

'Trust?' Her voice was harsh. 'Why should I trust you? We spent one night together. I don't recall *trust* being high on your agenda then.'

She clasped her hands, fingers twisting. The movement made her look young despite her expression of bored unconcern, making him recall his suspicion that she threw up defences to hide pain.

'Your eagerness to leave once you'd had your fill was downright insulting.' Her jaw angled high but didn't disguise the flush of colour across her cheekbones.

An answering rush of heat flooded his belly. Shame? He wasn't familiar with that emotion either.

Whenever he remembered that dawn confrontation, he focused on her disdain. It was easier to concentrate on that than the fact he'd bolted out of her bed, scared by the unaccustomed yearning that had filled him. It wasn't pressing business that had moved him, but the innate knowledge this woman was dangerous to his self-possession in ways he hadn't been ready to confront.

He hadn't stopped to think of her. Now he did.

'I shouldn't have left like that.'

A quick shrug told him it didn't matter to Marisa, but instinct told him she hid her feelings.

'I made a mistake.' Bright blue eyes locked with his and he read her shock, almost as strong as his own, that he'd admitted such a thing. 'But circumstances have changed. It's in both our interests to understand each other better.'

'Like you did at the party when you thought I was boozing and—'

'I was wrong.' His voice grew loud in frustration and he hefted in a deep breath, willing himself to be calm. This was unfamiliar territory but he was determined to see it through. Whatever it took to secure his child.

'I know you hide behind that smile of yours.' As he said it, Damaso realised it was true. How often on the trek had he seen her dazzling her audience with a smile? Yet when she was alone there was an air of sadness about her.

'You're an expert on me now, are you?' Her tone was accusatory but Damaso didn't take the bait. He had her measure, realising instinctively she'd try to alienate him rather than let him close.

But he wanted to be close. How else could he get what he wanted?

'No,' he said slowly, feeling his way. 'But I know the woman the press talks about isn't the real you. I know that far from being shallow you have unplumbed depths.'

It had taken him too long to realise that. His thinking had been muddled by emotion—something new and unfamiliar. Now the inconsistencies that had puzzled him coalesced into a fascinating whole.

How would a woman who was nothing but a shallow socialite have the patience for painstaking photography? He'd seen it engross her in the rainforest and again on his private estate.

Why would such a woman be upset at not being able to work if all she wanted was to party?

Above all, why hadn't she jumped at the chance to marry a billionaire who could buy and sell her quaint little kingdom several times over?

He should have wondered about that when she'd had two full days in the city to shop and had come back to the apartment with just one purchase: the dress she wore tonight.

'I don't claim to know who you are, Marisa.' His voice was raspy with self-disgust at his slowness. 'But I want to.'

'You have a strange way of showing it.' Her clipped words bit into what passed for his conscience. 'You left me as soon as we got to the party.'

It was true. He'd thought it wise to give her space. He'd kept his distance, more or less, these last weeks because crowding her would be counterproductive. Look what happened that afternoon on the beach.

'You were nervous?' He frowned. Marisa was so confident, used to being at the centre of a throng.

'Not nervous. But it would have been nice…' She shrugged, her gaze sliding away. 'Forget it.'

'No.' He paced closer. 'Tell me.'

Her head swung up, her stare impaling him. 'Let's just say fielding pointed questions about our relationship and the pregnancy isn't the best way to relax among strangers.'

'Someone had the gall to ask you about that?' He'd been so caught up in his strategy of giving her the illusion of space he hadn't considered that. He'd believed her status as his guest would protect her.

Guilt squirmed anew in his belly.

What was wrong with him? Usually he was ahead of the game, not six steps behind.

'Not directly.' Her mouth and nose pinched tight. 'But indirectly...' She shrugged, stress plain in her taut frame. 'It wasn't the most comfortable evening.'

'I shouldn't have left you.'

One pale brow arched as if she didn't believe him, then she looked away. 'The fact you took me there, then ostentatiously left me to fend for myself, sent a very particular signal.' Her tone was bitter.

Damaso scowled. '*Who* dared to insult you?'

Her head jerked round and he caught a flicker of surprise in her stare.

'There was no insult,' she said, her voice clipped and her chin high. 'But some of the men—'

'I can imagine.' Damn it. He could imagine all too well.

He swiped a hand round the back of his neck, massaging knotted muscles. If he'd been thinking instead of trying to find the best way forward with Marisa he'd have realised: he'd inadvertently signalled she was fair game for any man on the prowl for a quick fling with a gorgeous woman.

And she was gorgeous. He couldn't drag his eyes from her.

But she wasn't available.

She was *his*.

'I'm sorry.' Ineffectual as they were, he couldn't stop the words rising again to his lips. 'I should have been with you.'

He wasn't used to taking responsibility for anyone but himself. Now he cursed his failure. This woman made him re-evaluate so much he'd taken for granted. It was discomfiting.

Marisa walked to the window, her straight back and

shoulders telling their own story. 'I'm used to fighting my own battles. Tonight was no different.'

But it was—because he'd put her in that situation.

He'd never known guilt or regret before Marisa.

He'd never felt half the things he felt around her.

The laugh would be on him if she knew. She thought his embrace on the beach had been a tactic to seduce her into marrying him.

The truth was he'd wanted Marisa since the day they'd met. He wanted her with a sharp, stabbing hunger that grew daily.

He wanted her body. But he wanted her company too. Her smile. Her attention.

He wanted to keep her safe.

He wanted…

'I'm not used to apologising.' His voice came from just behind her and she shivered as its dark richness slid through her, making a mockery of her defences. 'But, for what it's worth, I really am sorry. For *everything*.'

If she wasn't careful, Damaso would overwhelm her. Over the past weeks she'd seen glimpses in him of a man she could come to care for. Marisa fought desperately to keep her distance but part of her wanted to surrender, give up the fight and be persuaded to trust him.

His hand on her shoulder was firm but gentle and she found herself turning at his insistence. In the soft lighting his eyes were unreadable yet the intensity of his stare made something in her chest tumble over.

'I should never have put you in that situation.' His lips twisted in a grimace. 'I thought to give you a treat.'

'A treat?' Marisa breathed deep. 'I'm not a child.'

But that was how he viewed her. Not surprising, given her reputation. She'd been maligned and vilified and she hadn't exactly led the life of a nun. There'd been a time when living up to her reputation of partying every night had been her life. But she'd bored of it quickly.

'Believe me, Marisa.' His accent thickened deliciously as he stepped squarely into her personal space. 'I know you're not a child.'

Lightning jagged through her at the rough, seductive timbre of his voice. At the feel of his hand warm on her shoulder. He seduced her so easily. Desperation rose. How could she resist him when she wanted so badly to give in?

'I'm not an easy lay, either.' The words shot out as she fought the sizzle of excitement in her blood. If he'd had a fight with his girlfriend, he needn't think he could turn to Marisa to warm his bed.

'I know, *querida*.'

'You're just saying that. At the party—'

'At the party I couldn't see straight for jealousy.'

'Jealousy?' The word stunned her, stealing her voice.

To be jealous, he'd have to care about her. She'd done her homework via the Internet and knew Damaso had a notoriously short attention span when it came to lovers. He thrived on pursuit. He certainly didn't stick around long enough for possessiveness. Yet the idea of him caring, just a little, cracked open a frozen part of her heart. 'You don't have a jealous bone in your body.'

'Don't I?' His mouth turned down in a tight grimace as he loomed close, hemming her in.

'What about this one? It's held you close.' Damaso picked up her hand and placed it on his forearm. She felt his heat through his clothes.

'Or this one.' He slid her hand up his arm and across to his collarbone. Her palm tingled at the contact and tiny ripples of delight fluttered up her arm. 'You slept there, do you remember? Your head on me, your leg over my belly.'

Damaso's voice was hypnotic, drawing her into a place where nothing existed beyond the pair of them and the haze of desire clouding her mind. No, not just desire. A longing for the warmth and…contentment she'd found so briefly with him. She swallowed hard, feeling herself weaken.

'Don't, Damaso.' She yanked but he wouldn't release her hand. Her heart hammered high in her throat as she fought panic.

'Why don't you go to your girlfriend?' Marisa hated the tell-tale way her voice wobbled. It revealed how much she cared.

'She's not my girlfriend.' His ebony gaze captured hers and her breath stalled. 'She stopped being that before I met you. Besides, I have no desire for any other woman.' The way he said it, as if the truth throbbed in his husky tones, made Marisa's knees turn to water.

'Stop it! Don't play these games.' She hated that he could make her feel so vulnerable, so hurt. So needy.

His other hand cupped her jaw, his touch gentle.

'I never play games, Marisa. Ever. Ask anyone—it's not my way.'

'Of course you do.' Her voice was half an octave too high. Was it his touch that did that? Or the fixed way he stared at her mouth? Or the searing tide of need rising inside? She jutted her chin.

'You tried to seduce me just days ago so I'd agree—'

His hand slid over her lips. She breathed in the fresh, salt scent of him, tasted it on her tongue when she swallowed. Why did it affect her so?

'And you told me not to touch you unless I meant it.'

Finally he dragged his hand away but, instead of releasing her, he spread long fingers over her throat, down to her collarbone, where her pulse hammered unevenly.

'I want you, Marisa.' He leaned in so the words caressed her face. 'You have no idea how much.'

She planted both hands on his wide chest and pushed. Nothing happened except her palms moulded to the solid shape of his torso.

'Don't lie. You only want me because I'm carrying your baby.' She'd never found a man she could trust. They were all out for something. And now it wasn't just her wellbeing at stake, but her unborn baby's. She had to keep a clear head for its sake and make the right decisions for its future. 'You want to secure me, that's all—trap me into marriage.'

Something dark and untamed glimmered in his eyes and Marisa's heart leapt against her ribs. Slowly, infinitesimally slowly, his lips curved into a smile that turned her insides to liquid fire. His hands slipped to her shoulders and, despite her caution, his touch on her bare skin melted another layer of her defences.

'It's true that I find the fact you're carrying my child unbelievably erotic.' His voice was husky and inviting. She'd never heard anything so mesmerising.

Damaso moved, one thigh wedging hers apart and pushing up against her. She gasped as she came in contact with his erection. Her inner muscles clenched needily, making a lie of her resistance.

His Adam's apple rose and fell as if he was nervous. Yet she was the one whose nerves were stretched to breaking.

'I mean it this time, Marisa. I want you. I've wanted you from the moment I saw you.' His chest rose as he drew in a shuddering breath. 'This is about more than the baby, or what the world thinks. This is about me and you. Right now, all I care about is how you make me feel, and how I make you feel.'

Despite everything, she wanted to believe him. How she wanted to!

He plucked one of her hands from his chest and planted a kiss at the centre of her palm. Her knees buckled as he sucked at her flesh, sending waves of weakness through her.

'Can't we forget tonight and start again?' His voice was dark, liquid temptation.

'Why?' Marisa clung to his shoulder for support, trying to shore up the distrust that would keep her and her child safe. 'What is it you want?'

'I want us to be just Damaso and Marisa. Simply that.'

Did he have any idea how perfect that sounded? How *real* and uncomplicated? How tempting?

Damaso's head swooped low and, with a sigh, Marisa gave up the battle she'd been losing for so long.

CHAPTER EIGHT

THIS TIME WHEN Damaso bent to kiss her, Marisa lifted her mouth to him, desire filling her. For the first time she didn't turn aside so his lips brushed her face, her throat or the sensitive point behind her ear.

The sensation of his mouth on hers, sure and hard, demanding the response she could no longer stop, blasted her into another world.

Wave upon wave of pleasure crashed through her. She clung to broad shoulders as his marauding mouth demanded more, ever more. Her surrender elicited a growl of satisfaction from Damaso that she felt right through her core as he gathered her close.

She needed this, him, filling her senses, as she couldn't remember needing anything in her life.

Even the night they'd shared—giving in to instinct and reaching out to Damaso in the hope he was different from the rest—Marisa had shied from this particular intimacy. She'd shared her body but kissing on the mouth had been a step too far. It was a boundary she hadn't crossed since Andreas had seduced and betrayed her. In her mind, it had become a symbol of gullibility and defeat.

Yet now she revelled in Damaso's hot, delving kiss, the tangle of tongues and hot breath, the flagrant openness and hunger.

There was no trace of bitterness, only the spicy, addictive taste of Damaso spinning her senses out of control and a thrill almost of triumph in her effervescent blood.

There was something else she couldn't name, something strong and pure, that filled her with elation and wonder.

This felt *right*. More than right.

She gave up trying to put a name to it as her mind fogged.

Marisa clamped her hands to the back of Damaso's head, revelling in the tangle of his thick, soft hair between her fingers. She angled her head to give him better access as he devoured her. His big hands held her close, his body anchoring her.

If this was defeat, it was glorious.

This kiss wasn't like Andreas's practised moves. Nor was it like Damaso's earlier attempt to seduce her into compliance. It was potent, hungry, untamed and it affected them both equally.

She felt the shudders rake Damaso's big frame as she moved against him; heard the raw delight in his gasp as she licked into his mouth; registered the convulsive tightening of his hands at her waist as she pressed even closer, trying to meld herself with him.

The air sizzled with the charge they generated.

Marisa wasn't surprised when a flash of light flickered across her closed eyes and a boom that could only be thunder ripped open the night. It was as if the elements had been triggered by the force of passion unleashed when Damaso set his mouth on hers.

Something cool and hard hit her bare shoulders; Damaso held her pinioned against the reinforced glass wall that gave such a spectacular view of the city. The cool glass made her even more aware of the intense heat of Damaso's aroused body. He was like a furnace.

Greedily, she wanted that heat for herself.

She dropped her hands to his shoulders and pushed his jacket back. He growled again, low in his throat, as if annoyed at the interruption, but let her go long enough to shake free of the jacket.

When he reached for her an instant later his hands moulded her breasts and she choked on a sigh of satisfaction.

'Yes! That!' Her head arched back against the glass, her breasts thrusting up into his palms as he caressed her, gently at first, then demandingly.

A guttural murmur broke from Damaso's throat. She didn't understand the Portuguese but her body responded to the urgency in his voice.

Her fingers fumbled at his collar, yanking at buttons till her hands met hard flesh. She wanted to bury her face there and taste the salty tang that rose sharp in her nostrils. She was wrestling with another button when Damaso's hands dropped away and she had to bite down hard to stop the mew of disappointment that rose on her lips.

She needed his touch on her body.

She wanted...

With one tremendous heave of shoulders and arms, Damaso ripped his shirt wide, buttons spattering to the floor. In the semi-dark Marisa watched the play of heavy muscles, the ripple of movement all the way down his dark, gold torso as he fought to tear the sleeves away.

Then he was bare-chested, snatching her hands in his and planting them high on his solid pectorals. Her palms tingled as hot flesh and the brush of body hair tickled.

'You're stunning,' she murmured. 'How did you get to look so good?'

He shook his head, his features taut as if fired in metal. 'It's you who's stunning, *querida*. I've never known a more perfect woman.'

'I'm not—'

Damaso's index finger closed her lips and it was a sign of her need that her tongue streaked out to taste him. His eyelids drooped as she licked him and the flesh beneath her hands rippled in spasm.

She did that to him so easily?

'You're perfect for *me*, Marisa.' His voice, thick with that sexy accent, brooked no argument. 'You're exactly what I want.'

Why that statement stilled her soul, Marisa didn't know.

Surely this was about lust? But when Damaso watched her like that, spoke of wanting her and only her, her heart gave a strange little leap. That look, those words, spoke to a part of her she'd kept hidden most of her life—the part that craved love.

'Stop thinking,' he growled, but his touch was gentle as he raised his hands and pulled the pins from her hair so it fell around her bare shoulders, a sensual caress that made her shiver. 'This is just you and me—Marisa and Damaso. Yes?'

His breath warmed her face; his hands dropped to her shoulders then down to the exquisitely tender upper slopes of her breasts. His fingertips traced the sweetheart neckline of her strapless dress, centimetre by slow centimetre, till she could take no more and clapped her hands over his, dragging them down to cup her breasts as she leaned close.

'Say yes, Marisa.'

She licked dry lips and through slitted eyes saw his gaze flicker.

'Yes, Damaso.'

It didn't matter whether she was saying yes to his statement that he wanted her, or his demand to stop thinking. Or whether she was simply urging him not to end the magic shimmering like stormy heat between them.

Whatever this was, she needed it, treasured it. For the first time in her life she felt not just passably pretty but beautiful, inside and out. No one had ever made her feel like this.

She blinked, her mouth hitching up in a tremulous smile

as a glow filled her that had nothing to do with the warmth of Damaso's body or the sultry night.

'Marisa.' His lips touched hers. Outside another crash of thunder shook the air, but it was the tenderness in Damaso's bass voice that made her quake. She leaned into him, her face upturned, her mouth clinging to his. He plunged one hand into her hair, holding her to him as he slowly, thoroughly, savoured the taste of her.

How could a kiss make her weak at the knees? She wobbled in her high heels, clutching Damaso for support.

She half-expected to see a satisfied smile at her reaction when he drew back. Instead she read nothing but taut control that made his features severe.

Then he was gone, dropping silently to his knees before her, hands knotting in the spangled froth of her skirt. She shivered as his hands slid up her bare legs, pushing the fabric up and up. Ripples of excitement shivered along her thighs. She pressed them together as she felt a rush of liquid desire.

Damaso lifted her shirt higher, then higher still, pausing when he saw the little silk bikini panties in aqua that she'd chosen to go with her new dress.

The sight of his dark head close enough for his breath to heat her skin like a phantom touch made excitement twist inside.

He pushed the fabric right up to her breasts, baring her to his gaze.

Marisa's breath laboured. There was something indescribably erotic about the way Damaso knelt at her feet, studying her so intently.

One large hand spread across her stomach, gently stroking till the tide of pleasure rose even higher.

'You're carrying our child in there.' He looked up, midnight eyes transfixing her. Before Marisa could think of anything to say, he leaned in and pressed a kiss to her flesh, then another and another. And all the while his eyes held hers.

She felt…treasured, vulnerable, different. The look on his face, the tenderness of his touch, the raw curl of arousal in her belly, created a moment of rapt awareness. She was a goddess come to life, the embodiment of femininity: creator, mother and seductress combined.

In that moment she felt awe at the miracle happening inside her and an unexpected sliver of hope. Damaso's reaction was genuine. Could this pregnancy really help them forge a relationship?

Damaso's mouth curved up in a smile. His eyes glittered in the soft light as he slid his hand down to the delicate silk of her panties, then with one swift tug dragged them down.

Over the sound of her gasp Marisa heard the whisper of tearing silk. Soft fabric fluttered down her legs.

'They were new!' Could he tell that was a gasp of anticipation, not outrage?

Damaso's smile widened. 'They were in the way.'

Before she could think of a retort, he dipped his head and her body convulsed as he pressed his lips to the centre point of every nerve. One stroke of his tongue and the trembling in her legs became a quaking shudder.

'Damaso!' Her fingers knotted in his hair, holding on, torn between wanting to pull him away and wanting him never to stop. For the storm was inside her now, the blasts of white-hot light jagging right through her again and again until, with a sob of shock, she shattered.

Marisa was tumbling, falling through a darkened sky lit by flashes of brilliant sparks. But she didn't fall. She was cushioned, wrapped close, gentled as she shuddered again and again, her body strung out on ecstasy.

A hand brushed her face and, dazed, she felt wetness. Marisa gulped in air and realised there were tears trickling down her cheeks.

She felt like she'd never recover from the surge of energy that had wracked her. More than delight, this was euphoria.

'I've never…' Her throat closed. How could she explain the depth of what she'd felt—the combination of sensual pleasure and emotional crisis that had created a perfect storm?

'Shh, *minha querida*. It's all right. I have you safe.'

And he did. Even in her bemused state she knew he protected her. Damaso's warmth and strength encompassed her, cocooning her. She burrowed closer, hands clinging.

She sank into soft cushions and Damaso eased away.

'No!' She clutched at him, hands sliding on his solid shoulders. 'Don't leave me.'

'I don't want to crush you.'

Marisa tried and failed to find the energy to lift her eyelids. 'I need you.'

Had she really said that?

For a moment there was no response. Then her limp body was picked up again and she found herself draped across Damaso. He was long and hard and spectacularly aroused.

'Sorry.' Her leg brushed his erection through his trousers and he tensed.

'It's okay. Just relax.'

That was new in her experience of men, she realised foggily. He really *was* putting her first.

She snuggled closer and he tensed, his hands clamping tight as if to stop her moving. Her head was pressed to his chest and she inhaled the delicious scent of his skin. She pressed a kiss there and felt a quiver ripple through him.

Marisa's exhaustion ebbed. She opened her eyes to a close-up view of Damaso's shoulder and taut biceps as he cradled her. She touched the tip of her tongue to his skin, tasting that curious combination of potent male and sea spice.

'Don't!'

'Why not?' She slipped her hand down to cover the heavy bulge in his trousers. His guttural response was part protest, part approval as he jerked hard beneath her.

'Because you're not ready.'

Marisa looked down to see his hand hovering over hers, as if he wanted to pull her away but couldn't quite manage it. She rubbed her hand up his length and saw his fingers clench. Beneath her ear, Damaso's heartbeat quickened.

She smiled. Now the power was hers. 'Let me be the judge of that.'

Deliberately she leaned over and licked his nipple, drawing it into her mouth.

Seconds later she was flat on her back on the sofa, pressed into the cushions by Damaso's big frame. Between them his hand scrabbled at his belt and zip. His other hand caught one of hers above her head.

His mouth closed with hers and this kiss was hunger and heat. It was utterly carnal, Damaso's tongue thrusting and demanding as he pushed her down into the soft upholstery. Wild elation rose as Marisa met each demand and added her own.

She needed Damaso to make her whole. Despite her shattering climax, there was an emptiness at her core only he could fill.

She was gasping when he surged back, rising to strip the last of his clothes and kick his shoes away.

Deep within, every muscle tightened as she surveyed Damaso, bronzed and powerful. Then he moved, shoving her legs wide, settling between them; his arms braced beside her, his breath warm on her lips, his eyes glittering as they ate her up.

He lay still so long she wondered if he'd changed his mind. Or was he waiting to see if she had?

Marisa reached down and took him in her hand, hot silk over rigid strength, and he shuddered.

In one fluid movement he dragged her hand away and

thrust slowly to the place she needed him. Her breath expelled in a sigh.

He moved again, sure and unhurried, as if savouring every sensation.

Next time he withdrew, Marisa tilted her hips, but instead of pressing deeper or harder Damaso took his time, centimetre by slow centimetre.

He was killing her. From complete satiation just minutes ago, remarkably now Marisa trembled with the need for more. She opened her mouth to urge him on then shut it as she registered his knotted brow, hazed in perspiration, the tendons tight to snapping point in his neck and arms, his gritted teeth.

This was killing him too!

'I won't break,' she gasped as he eased away and stroked gently back, teasing her unbearably with the need for more.

His eyes snapped open and she wondered if he saw her clearly. His gaze looked blind.

She planted her hands on his buttocks, feeling the twitch and bunch of muscle as she tried to draw him close, yet he resisted.

His eyes focused and her heart thudded at the look he gave her. Slowly he shook his head. 'The baby.'

He was afraid for the baby?

Marisa blinked. Emotions surged, engulfing her in a pool of warmth. At first she'd told herself she wasn't ready to have a child. More, she was scared about the responsibility of motherhood. But now she knew a certainty as deep as primitive instinct—that she wanted this child and would do anything to protect it.

And so would Damaso. This was connection at a visceral level, more profound than anything she'd ever expected.

He genuinely cared. He'd opened his heart to their unborn baby.

Could he open his heart to her too?

Something fluttered in her chest, her heart throbbing

too fast. A wave of emotion swept her, tumbling her into depths where the only anchor point was Damaso.

Hers. A voice in the deep murmured he was hers.

'The baby will be fine,' she whispered, wondering at the enormity of what she felt.

'How do you know?'

From instinct as old as time.

Marisa guessed he wouldn't be convinced by that. She focused on something more tangible. 'The doctor told me.'

Damaso breathed deep, his body sinking into hers. 'Still…' He shook his head, moving so slowly it was exquisite torture.

He was so obstinate, yet how could she protest when he thought to protect something so precious?

Marisa slipped her hands to his shoulders and hauled herself higher, nuzzling his jaw, kissing his ear, feeling the friction of his chest against her tender breasts. His breathing drew ragged

'I want you now,' she whispered, and bit down hard at the curve between his tanned neck and shoulder.

Damaso juddered, surging hard and high.

'Yes, like that.'

'Marisa.' It was a warning that became a groan as she wrapped her legs tight around him. For an instant he held strong, then his control broke and he surged into her, driving them hard and fast in a compulsive rhythm.

Marisa hugged him tight, filled with a feeling of openness, of protectiveness, as the big, powerful man who'd taken over her world let go and gave himself up to the force of passion.

Sex with Damaso had been spectacular.

Making love with him was indescribably better.

Marisa cradled him, overwhelmed by the belief they had shared something profound. Then, as their rhythm spun out of control, he bent to suckle her breast and both shattered in a climax that tumbled them into a new world.

CHAPTER NINE

THE STORM HAD PASSED, and the steady drum of rain should have lulled Damaso to sleep, yet it eluded him.

Staying with Marisa was too distracting. The rumpled disarray of the guest bedroom, the first one he'd staggered to with her in his arms, proved that.

He'd promised himself he wouldn't touch her after that cataclysmic coming together in the sitting room. He'd assured himself he could hold back from the need to imprint himself on her, taste and hold her. But his willpower had snapped when she'd turned to him again.

He hoped she and the doctor were right. Logic told him sex wouldn't harm the baby, yet he'd felt a profound fear of doing the wrong thing until Marisa had touched him.

He flung up an arm over his head, staring at the dark ceiling. His resolve had been renowned, and unbreakable, until her.

How had she done it? How had she overridden his determination to be gentle?

This wasn't what he'd planned. Granted, he'd wanted her in his bed. What better way to bind her to him than with sex? He'd use any tactic he could to convince her marriage was best.

But now he had her where he wanted her, Damaso realised things weren't so simple.

Tonight hadn't felt like any sex he'd had before.

It hadn't felt like he was in control.

On the contrary, his loss of control had been spectacular.

Then there was the way he'd *felt*. When he'd realised he'd hurt Marisa with his easy assumptions. When he'd knelt and kissed the woman who carried his baby. When she'd come apart so completely, her vulnerability had unravelled something inside, something he couldn't mend.

Each time he'd climaxed, it seemed he'd lost a little of himself in her.

He shifted. That was nonsense.

'Damaso?' Her drowsy voice was like rich, dark honey, sweet and enticing, making his mouth water.

He remembered being twenty-two, a kid from the slums who'd dragged himself into the commercial world with a mix of relentless determination, hard work and luck. He'd put his past behind him and thought he knew it all: how to turn a quick deal, where to find profits, how to satisfy a woman, how to protect himself on streets so much safer and more respectable than the ones he'd known.

He'd been in a breakfast meeting at a hotel. Damaso had followed the other man's lead, eating as they talked so as not to look too eager. He'd taken a bite of bread slathered in honey and had been instantly addicted.

Such a simple thing that most people took for granted. Yet just a taste had the power to drag him straight back to his past, deprived and wanting. To a time when honey had been a luxury he'd only heard of.

'Damaso?' Her hand touched his chest. 'What's wrong?'

He mentally shook himself out of abstraction. 'Nothing.' He paused, realising how abrupt he sounded. 'You must be tired. You should sleep.'

Her hand shifted, fluttering over his ribs, and he sucked in a breath as arousal stirred.

'Would you hold me?' She sounded tentative, unlike the feisty woman who'd faced him down time and again.

Did the past haunt her too?

How little he knew of her.

Silently he reached out and dragged her close, hoisting her leg over his and pushing her head onto his chest. Then he pulled the sheet over them both.

Holding her in his arms felt surprisingly satisfying. She was soft and serene and fitted snugly against him, as if designed for this. His breathing evened to a slow, relaxed rhythm.

'I should never have left you alone at the party.' Naked against him, he realised how tiny she was. She might have energy to burn, and an attitude the size of São Paolo, but that didn't mean she could take on the world alone.

'You've already said that.' Her mouth moved against his chest.

He had, hadn't he? It wasn't like him to dwell on mistakes. Yet he couldn't shake the guilt that he'd made her a target for unwanted attention.

'Nevertheless, I'm sorry. You—'

'Forget it, Damaso. I handled it.'

Damaso firmed his mouth rather than blurt that she shouldn't have needed to handle it.

'I'm sorry I lost my temper with you in public.' She puffed out a breath that warmed his skin. 'That will just fuel public interest.'

An apology from Marisa, too? Perhaps they *were* making progress. Damaso stroked a hand along her spine, enjoying its sensuous curve and the way she arched ever so slightly in response.

'Don't apologise. I should have known better.'

'What? Known I wasn't busy seducing other men and generally behaving badly?' Marisa's voice was a whisper yet he heard the tinge of bitterness she couldn't conceal. 'How could you? That's what everyone expects. It's in all the gossip magazines.'

She lay taut in his arms, that delicious lassitude replaced by tension. Damaso wished now he'd never raised the subject. But he owed her.

'The magazines are wrong.'

'I'd rather not discuss it.' She shifted as if to pull away and he wrapped both arms around her, holding her gently but firmly.

'I *know* they're wrong.'

Marisa stilled. 'You can't know that.'

'But I do.'

'Don't!' She twisted in his hold and he saw her pale face look up at him in the darkness. 'You don't need to pretend.' Her voice was scratchy and over-loud and it made something inside him ache.

'I don't know the details, Marisa. Only you do. But I do know you're not the woman the media paints you.' He paused, wondering how much he should admit. Then he registered the tiny shivers running through her taut frame and went on. 'I believed it at first but the more time I spent with you the more I came to realise you're someone quite different.' He ventured a caress along her bare shoulder. 'Someone I want to know.'

It was true. Marisa intrigued him. More than that, he'd discovered he *liked* her, even when she was prickly and refused to give in to his wishes.

'Why don't you tell me about it?' he murmured.

'Why would I do that?' No mistaking the wariness in her voice.

'Because you're hurting, and talking about it might make you feel better.'

His words surprised even himself. Not that he didn't mean them. It was how much he meant them, how much he wanted to help, that made him frown.

Since when had he been there for anyone? He was a loner. He'd never been in a long-term relationship. He didn't dwell on feelings. Yet here he was, offering a sympathetic ear as if he was the go-to guy for emotional support.

Yet he was sincere.

Another first.

If he wasn't careful this woman would change his life. Already she had him re-thinking so much he'd taken for granted.

'Why? Because you're such a good listener?' Marisa forced lightness into her tone but it didn't quite mask her pain. Her restless fingers moved over his rib cage until he clamped his hand over hers, spreading it wide against his chest. He liked her touch on him.

'I have no idea.' He didn't bother to add he'd never been anyone's confidant. 'Why don't you try me?'

He said no more but waited, slowly stroking the luxurious softness of her hair from her head down her back.

Marisa's words, when they came, surprised him.

'I was fifteen when the press came after me the first time.' Her voice was firm but a little breathless, as if she couldn't fill her lungs. Damaso forced himself to keep up the rhythm of his long strokes.

'There'd been press attention before then, of course. It was inevitable, with us orphaned when we were only ten. Every time we appeared in public they went into a frenzy—the poor little orphan royals.' Bitterness laced her words. 'Not that anyone cared enough to check we were all right.'

Damaso digested that in silence. He knew Marisa's relationship with her uncle, the current king and former regent, was poor, but better not to interrupt her with questions.

She drew a slow breath. 'Things eased a little over the years. Stefan and I got used to the media presence. Then at fifteen I was trying out for the national gymnastics team and suddenly I was in the spotlight again, initially because of the novelty of me competing with "ordinary" girls, and then…'

Damaso waited.

'Someone with an axe to grind fed them a story that I was a slut, partying all night with one guy after another, then playing the privileged prima donna among the rest of the competitors by day.'

'Who was it?'

'Who was what?'

'The person who invented the story.'

She lifted her head and even in the darkness he knew she searched his face. 'You believe me?'

'Of course.' It hadn't occurred to him she might lie. Everything about her, from her repressed emotion to her obvious tension, proclaimed the truth. 'Besides, I doubt you'd have the energy for bed hopping during the competition. Plus, you're anything but a prima donna, despite your pedigree.'

He'd watched her play the icy aristocrat when it suited, but he'd also seen how open and accessible she was to everyone on their tour. In his home she treated his staff with courtesy and genuine friendliness.

Marisa fisted one hand on his chest and propped her chin on it, staring.

'What?' He couldn't read her expression, but felt her gaze like the rasp of sharp metal on his flesh.

'You're the first person apart from Stefan and my coach to believe me.' Her voice had a curious, flat tone that he knew hid more than it revealed. He wondered how it had felt being vilified so publicly at such an age.

At least she'd had her brother.

'Surely your uncle's PR people would have helped?'

Marisa turned, lying again on her side, her face obscured. 'You'd have thought so, wouldn't you?'

Damaso waited, curious.

'They were spectacularly ineffective. But my uncle had never approved of my passion for gymnastics. He thought it unladylike and definitely not suitable for a royal. He disapproved of me being seen in leotards, getting sweaty and dishevelled in public, and especially on live TV. And as for competing with commoners!'

'He ordered his staff not to support you?' Damaso frowned. He knew how hard elite athletes worked. One of his few peers to succeed and, like him, make a life outside the slum where they'd grown up had gone on to represent Brazil at football. He'd seen how much dedication and hard work that took.

Marisa shrugged, her shoulder moving against his chest. 'I never found out. Eventually the gymnastics committee decided it was too counter-productive having me on the team. The press attention was affecting everyone. A week after I turned sixteen, I was dropped from the squad.'

Damaso fought the urge to wrap his arms tight around her. The fact that her voice was devoid of emotion told its own story. His chest tightened.

'Mighty convenient for your uncle.' Had he used the negative press stories to push his own ends?

'That's what Stefan said.' Bitterness coloured Marisa's words. 'But we could never prove anything, no matter what we suspected.'

Damaso stared into the darkness, putting two and two together. He recalled her hatred of the current king, the way even talking with him on the phone had sapped her energy. He remembered her comment about no one bothering to check she and her brother had been well-cared-for once Cyrill had become their guardian. That level of resentment must have deep roots. Was it possible her uncle had actually fostered the press stories?

'It's too late to worry about that now.' She did a good job of sounding matter-of-fact but he heard the undercurrent in her voice.

'Because the damage is done?'

'Sometimes it doesn't matter if a reputation is deserved. It takes on a life of its own.' She shifted against him. 'You'd be amazed how much difference a provocative caption can make to an innocent photo. Anything that didn't fit was seen as me or the palace trying to put a good face on things.'

'So you couldn't win.'

Abruptly Marisa tugged her hand free of his grip and

sat up, her back to him. She anchored the sheet beneath her arms and took her time pushing her hair back from her face.

'I survived.' Her tone was light. 'In fact, being known as a party girl made it easier to flout convention when the fancy took me, which it did. Eventually I learned to enjoy the benefits of notoriety, so it's not all bad. I always get invited to the most *interesting* parties.'

Damaso propped himself on one elbow, trying to read her profile in the darkness. He guessed her physical withdrawal meant he was getting too close for comfort.

Instinct told him Marisa wasn't used to sharing confidences either. She was strong and self-reliant in a way he recognised in himself, despite their dissimilar backgrounds.

Which meant it was time to back off. She didn't want him probing further.

Fat chance. He wanted to know all there was to know about her.

Besides, despite her tone of unconcern he sensed a fragility that intrigued him.

'Except you wanted something more. You said the other day you'd wanted to work but the press exposure stopped you.'

Had she stiffened or did he imagine it?

Her shoulders rose and fell in what passed for a shrug. 'It wouldn't have worked out anyway. I don't have any qualifications or useful skills.' Her chin lifted, reminding him of that morning in the jungle resort when she'd turned from beddable siren to haughty empress in the blink of an eye. Now, he'd swear it was a self-protection mechanism. Had it been that, then, too?

Marisa spoke, distracting him. 'I'm not academically minded. I barely made it through high school. Unless an employer wants someone who can make a perfect curtsey, or chat aimlessly with doddering aristocrats and bland-faced diplomats, my skills aren't exactly in demand.'

'Putting yourself down before someone else does it for you?'

That drew a reaction. She whipped round to face him, her hair flaring wide around her shoulders.

'Just facing facts, Damaso. I'm a realist.'

'Me too.' And what he saw was a woman who'd been badly hurt time and again but conditioned herself not to show it.

He should be grateful she didn't cry on his shoulder.

But he wasn't. Something wild and dark inside clawed with fury at the way she'd been treated. The way she'd been judged and dismissed.

He wanted to grab her uncle and the media piranhas by their collective throats and choke some apologies out of them.

He wanted to crush Marisa in his arms and hold her till the pain went away. She'd probably shove him aside for his trouble. Besides, what did he know of offering comfort?

'Let's end this conversation, Damaso. I've had enough.'

Yet he couldn't leave this.

'So you played up to your reputation. Who wouldn't in the circumstances? But we've already established you're not as promiscuous as the world thinks.'

'Don't forget the drug-taking and high-stakes gambling.' Even in the gloom he saw her chin jut higher.

Damaso tilted his head. Why was she raising those rumours? It was as if she'd changed her mind about sharing herself with him and took refuge instead in her reputation for licence.

'And did you? Snort coke and lose a fortune gambling?'

'I lost my driver's licence just two and a half months ago doing twice the speed limit on the hairpin bends above the palace.'

Two and a half months ago. 'After your brother died?'

'Leave Stefan out of this.' Marisa swung her legs out

of bed but Damaso's hand on her arm shackled her so she couldn't move.

'Let me go. I told you I'd had enough.' Her voice was clipped and condescending and a frisson of long-forgotten shame feathered his spine—as if he was still a ragged slum kid who'd dared to touch a princess with his dirty paw.

His hand gentled.

'You're too fit to be a regular drug user, Marisa. I've seen too many of them to be fooled. And as for gambling... You've had ample opportunity since you arrived but you've shown no interest.' He paused. 'That leaves your reputation with men.'

'I'm hardly a virgin, Damaso.'

For which he was grateful. Sex with Marisa was one of life's high points.

'So how many have there been, Marisa?'

She tugged at his arm but he held firm.

'You can't seriously be asking that.'

'I seriously am.'

For four pulse beats, five, six, she stared him down. Then she leaned towards him, her free hand sliding from his thigh to his groin, closing around his already quickening shaft.

'Enough.' Her voice was a throaty murmur that turned his bones molten.

'Convince me.'

For a flicker of a moment she hesitated. Then she shoved him back on the pillow and bent her head. Long tresses of silk caressed his skin. Her lips were hot and soft, wickedly arousing on his burgeoning flesh.

But something was wrong. Damaso felt the tension in her frame, as if her nerves had been stretched to breaking point.

With a groan of disbelief at what he was about to do, Damaso pushed her away, rolling her onto her back and imprisoning her with the weight of his body.

They lay so close he saw the over-bright glitter of her fine eyes and the uneven twist of her lips.

'Don't *ever* do that unless you want it too.' The idea of her servicing him rather than acting out of shared arousal left a bitter taste on his tongue. For that was what she'd been doing, he was sure of it—trying to distract him.

Slowly, tenderly, he leaned down and planted a kiss at the corner of her mouth, another near her nose, then across her cheek to follow a leisurely trail down her neck. By the time he reached the base of her throat, her pulse was frantic. He kissed her there, ridiculously reassured by this proof of her response.

Marisa wanted him. Had wanted him all along. It was just that she'd tried to side-track him to avoid answering questions.

His hand slipped between her legs as he moved lower to kiss her nipple. With a sigh she tilted her hips and he pressed harder, rewarding her responsiveness.

'How many men, Marisa?'

She stiffened, her indrawn breath a hiss in the darkness.

Damaso feathered teasing kisses across her breast, his fingers delving into her most sensitive place. Marisa's hands threaded through his hair, holding him close.

When she was soft again beneath him he stopped.

'How many?'

'You're a devil, Damaso Pires.'

'So I've been told.' He nipped gently at her breast and watched her arch high. 'How many?' Deliberately he lifted his hand away. Still Marisa didn't admit defeat.

It took ten minutes of delicious pleasure before she finally gave in, by which time Damaso was close to losing the last of his own control.

'Two,' she gasped, her body writhing beneath his.

'Two?' Damaso couldn't believe his ears. Only two men before him?

'Well…one and a half.' She drew him down till he sank between her thighs.

'How can there be a half?' He groaned when he found his voice. She was slowly killing him.

Marisa's eyes opened and for a moment he could have sworn he read pain in her eyes, though it should have been impossible in the darkness.

'The first one seduced me so he could brag about it to his friends. After that…' She looked away. 'After that I found it hard to trust, so the second one didn't get as far as he expected.'

Damaso braced himself high and joined them with one easy move that took him home. 'Not this far?'

'No.'

'But you don't mind…with me?'

Slowly she smiled and the tightness banding his chest fell away.

'I don't mind.' She gasped when he moved and clutched his upper arms. 'I could even…come to quite enjoy it.'

Quite enjoy it!

There was a challenge if ever he'd heard one.

Damaso made absolutely sure she'd more than 'quite enjoyed' herself before he was finished.

Finally she lay limp against him, curled up with her head tucked beneath his chin, her knee between his and her hand flung across him where it had fallen when he'd rolled onto his back.

Her breathing was deep and steady, and he told himself if she dreamed it was of something pleasant, not the disappointments and pain of her past.

Damaso was sure he had only half the story. But that was enough. Duped and betrayed by her first lover, hung out to dry by the uncle who should have protected her, scorned by the world's press… Who'd been on her side?

Her twin, Stefan, who'd died just months ago.

Damaso had assumed the passion he'd shared with

Marisa that first night was the product of two healthy libidos and a wildfire of mutual attraction. Yet he recalled the blind look on Marisa's face as she'd tackled that notorious climb on the trek. She'd been lost in her own world and the blankness of her stare had scared him. Had that been grief driving her?

Had grief pushed her into his arms?

He swallowed and turned his gaze to the first grey fingers of dawn spreading across the sprawling city.

She'd had only one real lover before him.

One!

Damaso would love to think it was his sheer magnetism that had made her walk into his arms. But did that ring true with a woman who'd guarded her lack of sexual experience under the eyes of the gloating world press? Who, even when she partied all night, kept herself apart from casual sexual encounters?

There'd been a wealth of pain in Marisa's voice as she'd spoke of the man who'd betrayed her. It made Damaso want to commit violence.

What had it done to her?

He'd thought Marisa sexy and alluring with a feisty, 'don't give a damn what society thinks' attitude that matched his.

Instead he'd discovered she was a woman who needed careful handling. She had so much front it was hard to tell where the public persona ended and the real woman began. One thing he knew for sure—behind her masks of hauteur and unconcern was a woman who felt, and hurt, deeply.

His fingers twitched as she shifted, her breath hazing his skin. He wanted her again with a hunger he found almost impossible to conquer.

If she'd been the woman he'd first thought, he'd have had no qualms about waking her.

Instead Marisa was a unique mix of fragility and

strength. A woman who, instinct told him, needed the sort of man he didn't know how to be.

For the first time in years, he felt inadequate. Tension made his jaw ache as he contemplated the tangle that was their relationship.

Damaso wasn't equipped to deal with the nuances of emotional pain. He'd experienced and witnessed so much trauma as a kid he'd all but excised feelings from his life until he'd met Marisa.

He didn't know how to give Marisa what she needed.

Her vulnerability made him feel like a clumsy lout who'd blundered in and smashed what was left of her fragile peace by getting her pregnant.

A better man would regret that.

A better man would support her yet let her go.

Damaso had never been anything like a good man. He was too used to getting his own way. He'd been driven solely by the need to survive, then thrive.

He couldn't bring himself to wish Marisa's pregnancy away. He was too selfish for that.

He wanted his child.

He wanted Marisa.

His hand tightened on her hip and he smiled grimly when she snuggled closer, as if this was where she wanted to be.

Who was he kidding? He'd seduced her, taking advantage of her vulnerability after the stress of the party. He'd used his superior sexual experience to make her open up to him, physically and emotionally.

And he'd continued to push his way into her life, inveigling her to become part of his.

A better man…

No, he'd never be a better man. He was hard, bent on winning at all costs.

His one concession would be that from now on, knowing what he did of Marisa's story, he'd treat her gently, give her space and time to adjust to her new life with him.

He'd learn what he needed to protect her and keep her with him till she wanted to stay by choice.

Even if it meant keeping his distance till she did.

CHAPTER TEN

'BUT YOU CAN'T have considered, Your Highness!'

Marisa leaned back in her cushioned seat and raised one eyebrow, knowing her silence would be like a red rag to a bull. She seethed at the superior attitude taken by the Bengarian ambassador. He was her uncle's crony, and no doubt Cyrill's belief that he could command and she'd obey had rubbed off.

'Think of the publicity,' he urged. 'Think of the gossip. You *have* to be there for the King's coronation.'

'I don't recall anything about that in the constitution.' She should know; she'd been force-fed the document as a child, reminded again and again of her royal obligations and all the ways she didn't measure up.

Languidly she crossed one leg over the other. The ambassador's gaze dropped to her bright sandals, then up past her linen trousers to the gauzy top in tropical shades of lime-green and vivid yellow that she'd picked up just last week in the markets.

No wonder he pursed his lips and frowned. She looked good, she reminded herself. In fact, she looked blooming. Obviously the early stages of pregnancy agreed with her now the sickness had passed. But, though she was dressed with casual chic, she'd refused to don the staid, formal clothes expected of a Bengarian princess.

She wasn't in Bengaria and had no intention of returning.

'If I may say, princess...' he paused long enough for

her to feel bile rise at that unctuous tone '...you have an obligation not only to your country but to your uncle, who sacrificed so much for you. Remember that he raised you.'

'And I'm the woman I am today because of him.' Let him chew on that for a while. When the ambassador simply frowned, she added, 'We've never been close. He'll hardly miss me in the throng.'

No doubt Cyrill would be surrounded by sycophants, people who had feathered their nests from the royal coffers.

'If I may say, Your Highness, that's a very...' He read her expression and paused. 'Unhelpful attitude.'

If he expected that to convince her, he had a lot to learn.

'I wasn't aware anyone expected me to be helpful.' She leaned forward a fraction. 'In fact, I seem to recall being advised months ago that it would be to the country's benefit if I left as quickly and quietly as possible.'

He had the grace to blush.

'Now.' She rose to her feet. 'Thank you for your visit. As always, it's a delight to be brought up to date with the news from Bengaria. But I'm afraid I've another appointment.'

'But you can't just—' She watched him swallow, his Adam's apple bobbing in that scrawny throat. She'd feel sorry for him if she didn't know him for one of Cyrill's yes-men who'd made Stefan's life and her own a nightmare obstacle course of deliberate disruption and sabotage. 'I mean.' He fiddled with his tie as if it were too tight. 'The baby.'

'Baby?' Marisa surveyed him with a glacial stare that would have done Cyrill himself proud.

'Your baby.'

Marisa said nothing. She had no intention of discussing her pregnancy with her uncle's envoy.

'King Cyrill had hoped... That is to say, he's already making arrangements...'

Arrangements to do what? Adopt out her child? Force her to have an abortion? Marisa's flesh crawled.

In the innermost recesses of her heart lurked a fear she might not have what it took to be a good mother. That she might let her child down. But despite her doubts Marisa would face down the King of Bengaria and the whole of his parliament before she let him lay a hand on her child.

'As ever, I'm fascinated by my uncle's plans.' She forced the words beyond the knot of fear in her constricting throat. 'Do tell.'

The ambassador shifted and cleared his throat.

Finally he spoke. 'The King has graciously decided to negotiate a royal match that will give your child legitimacy and save your reputation. He's been in discussion with the Prince of—'

Marisa flung up a hand and the ambassador lapsed into silence. Her stomach heaved as his words penetrated like arrows. This time it took almost a minute before she could speak.

'With someone who is willing to overlook the little matter of another man's child,' she murmured. 'In return for my uncle's help in shoring up his social position.' Her mouth twisted. 'Or is it his wealth? No, don't tell me, I really don't want to know.'

Cyrill must be desperate to contain any possible damage to the royal family's reputation. Or, just as likely, to have some positive media to counteract the negativity his harsh rule was attracting. There was nothing like a royal wedding and a royal baby to turn the tide of public opinion.

But not *her* baby!

Marisa would do anything to ensure her child wasn't a royal pawn. It would grow up as far from palace machinations as possible.

She was determined her child would have what she hadn't: love and a nurturing environment. She'd even begun to wonder if perhaps marriage to Damaso might provide that. He didn't love *her* but she had no doubt he cared for their baby.

Marisa drew a slow breath and dredged the depths of her strength. She felt ridiculously shaky but determined not to show it.

'You can thank my uncle for his concern but I'll be making my own arrangements from now on. Good day.'

Without a second glance, she turned and swept out of the room, the ambassador's protests a vague background babble over the sound of her rough breathing and the blood pulsing in her ears. If she didn't get to the bathroom soon…

'Madam, are you all right?'

It was Ernesto, Damaso's butler-come-bodyguard, assigned to accompany her whenever she went out. For the first time, she was truly thankful for his enormous height and sheer bulk.

'Please make sure the ambassador is escorted from the apartment.' She swallowed convulsively, feeling her insides churn uncomfortably, and pressed her hand to her mouth.

Ernesto hesitated only a split second, concern in his shrewd, dark eyes, then swung away.

'And make sure he doesn't return,' Marisa gasped.

'You'll never see him again, madam.' The bass rumble was ridiculously reassuring as she stumbled to the bathroom.

When she emerged Ernesto appeared with a laden tray.

'Thanks, but I'm not hungry.'

'If you've been unwell you need to replace your fluids. The mint tea will make you feel better.'

At Marisa's stare, he shrugged and put the tray on the coffee table. 'So Beatriz says.'

Great; he and the housekeeper were discussing her health now.

Yet the knowledge soothed rather than annoyed her. Ernesto and Beatriz, like Damaso's staff on the island, were unlike any servants she'd known. They genuinely cared about their employer and, by extension, her.

She wasn't used to being cared for. Stefan and she had shared a bond nothing could sever, but each had had their own pursuits and, once he'd become King, Stefan shouldered new responsibilities.

As for Damaso, Marisa was sure he cared. Look at the way he personally escorted her now to restaurants, dance clubs and parties, never leaving her side. Every night his tender seduction drew her more and more under his spell.

Damaso cared, all right. But whether for her or her baby, she wasn't sure.

She'd spilled her secrets to him, revealing details she'd never shared, and he'd held her and made love to her in such a way, she'd swear he understood.

And yet...

Marisa chewed her lip, confronting the doubts that had racked her since that memorable night when she'd given herself to him again. She'd opened up to Damaso in ways she never had with any man. The catharsis of reliving her past, and giving herself so completely, had left her limp and drained, yet more whole than she'd felt in years. Even the devastating loss of her twin seemed more bearable.

The next morning she'd woken with scratchy eyes and heavy limbs but to a sense of renewed hope. Until she'd found Damaso had left her to sleep late while he went to work.

What had she expected? That he'd stay with her, sharing his own secrets as she'd done hers?

She wasn't so naïve. Yet she'd hoped for *something*. Some breaking down of the barriers between them. At a physical level, the barriers had shattered, but emotionally? It felt like Damaso had retreated even further. She was no closer to knowing him than she'd been a month ago.

Oh, he was tender in bed, and solicitous when they went out. Her mouth twisted as she remembered how he'd staked his claim over her just last night at another exclusive party. Marisa wanted to believe it was because he felt something for her. But more likely he was doing what was necessary to get what he wanted—access to their baby.

The trouble was she longed to trust him as he urged, not just with her body but with her future and her child's. Even with her heart.

She sucked in a sharp, shocked breath.

How could she think like that? She'd loved two people in her life, her mother and her brother, and their deaths had all but shattered her. Loving was far too dangerous.

'Madam?'

Ernesto held out a steaming porcelain cup in his massive hand.

Dragged from her circling thoughts, Marisa accepted the cup. She was too wired to sit and eat the pastries Beatriz had prepared, but she'd learned to appreciate Brazilian mint tea. She lowered her head and inhaled, feeling a modicum of calm ease her tense body.

'I'll go out when I've had this.' She was too restless to stay indoors.

Ernesto nodded. 'By helicopter or car?'

It was on the tip of Marisa's tongue to say she wanted to walk, blocks and blocks through the teeming city. Anything to numb the pain and the trickle of fear the ambassador's words had stirred. Anything to blot out the fear that she was in danger of swapping one gilded cage for another.

She was safe from her uncle's machinations—he couldn't force her into an arranged marriage—but the fact remained she'd let weeks race by without coming up with a plan for her future and the baby's. She needed to decide where they'd live, not drift aimlessly.

A vision of Damaso's private island swam in her brain and her lips curved as she imagined splashing in the shallows with an ebony-haired toddler.

Marisa blinked and sipped her tea. Maybe it would soothe her need for action.

'Where is Damaso today?'

Stupid that her thoughts turned to him so often. He'd never pretended to care for her as anything more than the woman carrying his child. But this last week, despite logic, she'd imagined a deeper connection between them.

How could that be when he left her to her own devices all day? She told herself she was glad he found it so easy to push aside the intimacy of their nights together. Better than having him on hand, reminding her of his demand that they marry.

'He's out in the city.'

'In his office?' Damaso had pointed out the building to Marisa one night on their way to an exclusive club.

'No, madam.'

Ernesto's less than helpful answer made her prick up her ears. Or maybe it was because she sought distraction from her fears.

'I'd like to see him.' She watched over the top of the delicate cup as Ernesto's eyes widened a fraction.

'I'm not sure that's a good idea.'

'Why not?' What was Damaso doing that he wanted to keep from her? He was as close as a clam about his life.

Ernesto hesitated a moment. 'He's in one of the *favelas*.'

'*Favelas*?' Marisa was sure she'd heard the word before.

'Poor neighbourhoods. Where the houses aren't—' He shrugged, his English apparently failing him. 'A slum,' he said finally.

Marisa frowned. That was the last thing she'd expected. She put down her cup and saucer, relieved to have something to divert her from Cyrill's schemes. 'You can take me there.'

'Truly, madam, this isn't a good idea.'

Marisa smiled her sympathy at Ernesto as they negotiated a rutted dirt road, but refused to turn back. Not till she found Damaso and what had brought him here.

On either side of the track rose haphazard buildings,

some solid-looking and painted in bright colours, others looking like they'd been cobbled together with whatever materials could be salvaged. The scent of fires, spicy food and something much less savoury lingered in the air. Marisa plodded on. It wasn't the first place she'd visited that didn't have a reliable sewage system.

They approached a long building painted saffron-yellow and the bodyguards Ernesto had brought fanned out. Ernesto gestured for her to accompany him inside.

The first face she saw was Damaso's. He sat at a battered metal table with a group of men, all sipping coffee out of tiny cups, engrossed in conversation. His proud features were intent as he listened to an older man speak and he leaned back, as if fading into the background. Yet even in casual jeans and shirt he stood out from the rest.

Marisa's breath caught as she drank in the sight of him.

He didn't see her and she stopped just inside the open door, letting her senses adjust.

The building was cavernous. Over behind the men was an indoor basketball court where a bunch of gangly teens played, encouraged by catcalls and cheers.

From a door to the left came the clanging of pots and a delicious savoury scent that could only mean someone was cooking. Over on the far left, she heard music and voices, and straight ahead on a battered wall was tacked a collection of photos.

Instinctively she moved towards the photos, telling herself she hadn't lost her nerve about seeing Damaso. He was busy, and not with some dusky beauty as she'd half-feared.

Marisa wrestled with self-directed anger. Why had it been so imperative she see him? She could deal with her uncle's schemes without running to Damaso for support.

The photos ranged from ordinary snapshots to one or two that made her pulse trip a beat. That one of the skinny teenager, his eyes far too old for his face, his expression weary yet his stance all pugnacious machismo, as if he dared the world to mess with him. The wistful look on the old woman's crinkled face as she watched a young couple in bright colours dance on a cracked concrete floor, their bodies lithe and sinuous, the embodiment of sexual energy.

'What are you doing here, Marisa?'

'Admiring the art.' She didn't turn, preferring not to respond to Damaso's dark tone. 'Some of these are remarkable.'

'You shouldn't have come.' She heard him drag in a breath. 'Ernesto should have known better.'

'Don't blame Ernesto.' She turned and met his shadowed glare, wondering exactly what she'd interrupted. Damaso's tension was palpable. She'd never seen him so edgy. 'He didn't want to bring me here but his orders are to keep me safe, not a prisoner.'

Damaso's nostrils flared as he breathed deep, apparently searching for calm. He couldn't have missed the challenge in her tone. She'd agreed to stay with him, but on condition there was no coercion. Restricting her movements would violate that.

Marisa watched his hands bunch then flex, as if he resisted the urge to pick her up and cart her away. For a moment she was tempted to provoke him, break the invisible barrier that kept him so aloof while she felt impossibly needy.

Hurt and anger warred with pride. This wasn't the place.

'You think this place is safe?' Warning filled his voice.

'I have guards. Besides, you're here.' She didn't add that at least some of the locals had seemed friendly. She hadn't missed the wary looks of others and the way a few figures had skulked away into the shadows as they'd passed.

'That's different.'

Marisa tilted her head to one side, taking in his clenched jaw and the tight line of white around his mouth.

'I can see it is.' She wasn't a fool. 'But I was curious.'

'Now you've seen it, you can leave.'

That didn't even deserve a response. 'What is this place?'

Damaso shoved his hands into his pockets. 'A local gathering place. A community centre, if you like.'

'I'm sorry I interrupted your meeting.' She nodded to the group of seated men watching them.

'We'd finished. Now.' He reached out and took her arm, his hold implacable. 'It's time we left.'

'What are you hiding, Damaso?'

His head jerked back as if she'd slapped him and his gaze slid away. Marisa stared, stunned that her instinct had been right. He was concealing something.

Damaso's lips moved as if he were about to speak but he said nothing. His face took on that spare, hewn look that she'd come to suspect meant he repressed strong feeling.

Instinctively she covered his hand with her own.

'Now I'm here, won't you show me around?' She met his stare openly. 'It's important to you,' she said slowly, 'or you wouldn't be here.' For clearly this wasn't some high-powered finance meeting that would reap more profits for his ever-expanding empire. 'Please?'

His exhalation of breath was a warm gust on her face. 'You're not leaving till I do, are you?'

Marisa shook her head and felt the rock-solid muscle of his arm ease a little against hers.

'Very well.'

Damaso intended the tour to take a brief ten minutes but he'd reckoned without the inevitable interest Marisa aroused. People came out of the woodwork to see the gorgeous blonde Damaso Pires had brought into their midst.

As the clustering numbers grew, tension ratcheted up again. He couldn't believe she was in any danger with him. Yet he couldn't be comfortable with Marisa in these surroundings. It just wasn't right.

To her credit, Marisa wasn't fazed. She was interested in everything, not pushing herself forward, but not afraid to initiate conversation in her halting Portuguese that Damaso for one found endearing and sexy.

They loved her, drawn by her bright energy and enthusiasm. By the way she didn't shy from shaking hands and sharing a joke. By her interest, especially in the kids. Some girls had been having a dance class and showed what they'd learnt. When one, a little over-eager, stumbled when she attempted a cartwheel, Marisa showed her how to place her hands, shucking off her shoes and demonstrating, then helping the little one get the move right.

Damaso smothered a smile. It was the first time he'd seen his security staff lost for words. As for the kids, they regarded her with a mix of awe and acceptance that made him proud and infuriated at the same time.

'This is marvellous.' Marisa smiled up at the woman who'd served her at the large communal table and dipped her spoon back into the bowl that had been set before her. 'Tell me what it's called?'

'Feijoada—black bean stew.' Even now, with the budget to live on champagne and lobster, it was Damaso's favourite dish. In the days when he'd first eaten it, of course, there'd been very little meat to flavour the rich dish, and much more of the rice and beans.

'Do you think Beatriz would make it for us?'

He nodded. Beatriz, like he, had grown up with it.

One of the little girls sidled closer to Marisa on the long bench seat, her eyes wide. At a comment from Marisa in hesitant Portuguese, she grinned and began talking.

Damaso watched them communicate easily with so few words and felt something tighten and twist deep in his belly. He should have known Marisa would take a visit to a poor neighbourhood in her stride. As a princess, she was no doubt used to playing Lady Bountiful, bringing out that practised smile to charm the adoring crowds.

But this was something else. This wasn't stage-managed. He felt the warmth of her personality reach out and encompass him as it enthralled the little girl.

Yet some dark thing inside him rebelled at Marisa being here. It coiled through his gut, clawed through his veins and made him itch to drag her away to the world where she belonged. A world of luxury and ease, where he could take care of her while she nurtured the baby they'd created.

That was it. The baby.

She had to think of the baby's wellbeing, not salve her social conscience visiting the poor.

'It's time we left.'

He rose and held out his hand. Even to his own ears the words were abrupt and he saw startled looks directed his way.

The little girl shrank away as if he'd shouted at her and he felt heat score his cheeks as shame flared. But it couldn't counteract the terrible urgency gnawing at his innards. He had to get Marisa away from here. Now!

It took a lifetime for Marisa to move. His pulse galloped as he watched her turn and say something to the girl that made her grin shyly. Then Marisa rose from her wooden seat with all the grace of an empress. An empress who ignored his outstretched hand with a disdain that knifed right to his chest. Her gaze slid across his face before she turned and thanked first one person and then another for their hospitality.

They clustered around, responding to her warmth and sincerity, and absurdly Damaso felt locked out, as if he were alone in the darkness, cut off from a happiness he hadn't even known he'd grown accustomed to.

Absurd!

He was successful. Sought-after. He had it all, everything he'd ever dreamed of and more.

Yet when Marisa finally made a move to leave, turning not to him but to Ernesto, something fractured inside.

In two strides Damaso was at her side, tugging her arm through his. She stiffened and her smile grew fixed but she didn't pull away.

Good! He'd run out of patience.

CHAPTER ELEVEN

Neither spoke on the journey. He was reminded of the night of the party when he'd been jealous and suspicious, when she'd stood up to him and they'd come together in such a conflagration it had melted his self-control.

But this was different. This was… He shook his head, unable to put a name to the vast, nameless void that had taken up residence in this chest the moment he'd seen Marisa in the squalor that had been the only world he'd known.

Nevertheless, he held himself in check as they entered the apartment and Marisa headed to the bedroom they shared.

Did he expect her to pack her things? Was that the source of the tension knotting his belly?

But she merely dropped her bag on the bed and headed for the bathroom. His hand on the door stopped it closing behind her.

'I'd like some privacy while I take a bath.' Her eyes fixed on his left ear and turbulent anger rose in a coiling wave. He would *not* be dismissed.

'Since when have you needed privacy for that?' Deliberately he let his gaze rove her body, lingering on the swift rise and fall of her lush, pert breasts, the narrow waist that always seemed impossibly tiny beneath his hands and the delicious curve of her hips.

'Since now, Damaso.' She turned away, unclasping her

chunky silver bracelet and putting it on a tray beneath the mirror. 'I'm not in the mood for dealing with you.'

'*Dealing* with me?'

His gaze collided with hers in the mirror and he realised when she flinched that he'd shouted.

Her chin inched up as she took a silver and turquoise stud from her ear and let it clatter onto the tray.

'Your disapproval.' Her throat worked and something dragged at his belly, like a plough raking deep and drawing blood. 'You couldn't have made it any clearer that you don't want me meeting your friends. And don't try to tell me those people aren't important to you. Anyone could see they mean more than the social set you party with.'

Her hands worked at the other stud yet she couldn't seem to drag it free.

'But if you think you can just dismiss me as not good enough because I don't have a vocation or a career, because I haven't yet made anything of my life, then you can think again.' Her voice wobbled and the raw furrow in his belly gaped wider, sucking his breath out as pain stabbed.

'I don't—'

'I don't want to hear it, Damaso. Not now.' Finally she loosened the earring and it clattered onto the tray then bounced to the floor. Marisa didn't notice. 'Not while I'm trying to decide whether to leave.'

Her gaze dropped to her watch as she fumbled with the band.

Damaso didn't realise he'd moved till he saw his hand reach out and brush her fingers aside.

He swallowed down a toxic brew of self-disgust and anger as he unclasped her watch and placed it on the crystal tray with her jewellery.

'I don't want you to leave.' For a miracle, the words emerged steadily. He told himself Marisa was grieving and insecure. She'd misunderstood his actions. There was no danger of her leaving. He'd stop her, one way or another.

She shook her head and tendrils of spun gold feathered her cheeks. 'It's too late for that.' She put a hand to his chest and shoved.

As if that would move him. For all her energy, she was tiny. He captured her hand in his, pressing it hard against his chest.

'Marisa, you've got it wrong.' Damaso searched his brain for an explanation. That was it: the child. 'You have to be careful of the baby. In an area like that—'

'Stop it! I don't want to hear any more.' The way her voice suddenly rose silenced him. He'd never heard Marisa so…desperate.

She drew a shuddering breath. 'I know the baby is ultimately all you care about, Damaso, but don't try to dress up what happened today.' Her eyes met his, boring right into his soul. 'You disapproved of me being there because you disapprove of me. It was plain as the nose on your face.'

He saw the bright sheen of her eyes and knew he was on the verge of losing her.

'Disapprove of you?' His laugh was harsh. 'You have no idea.' He crowded her back against the vanity unit, his hands running over her as if learning her body's shape all over again, or ensuring she was whole and unscarred by today's outing.

'Don't try to seduce me, Damaso. It won't work. Not this time.'

He shook his head as he searched for the right words.

'I didn't want you there. It's not safe. It's not…' The words dried as his throat constricted. How could he explain that awful blank fear that had consumed him, seeing her there? His hands balled into straining fists. 'You shouldn't be in such a place.'

'I might have been born a princess, Damaso, but I don't live in an ivory tower.'

'You don't understand.' He hefted a deep breath that didn't fill his lungs. 'It's too dangerous.'

'For the baby. So you say.'

He gripped her shoulders and her startled eyes met his. 'Not just the baby. You too.' He ground the words out past a clenched jaw. 'You have no idea what can happen in a place like that. I needed to protect you, get you away from there.'

His breath sawed loud and fast, competing with the drumming blood in his ears. He knew he held her too tight but he couldn't get his hands to relax.

'What can happen, Damaso?' Her quiet voice penetrated the thunder of his pulse. Her eyes held his and for the first time he had her full attention. Maybe she'd listen now.

Her hand touched his cheek and the delicacy of it against his unshaven jaw reminded him of all the differences between them. Differences he'd ignored until today, when their two worlds had collided with shattering impact.

The palace and the slum.

'Too much.' His voice was hoarse as he ran his hands up and down her back, reassuring himself she really was all right. 'Disease, danger, violence.'

'Those people live there every day.'

'Because they have to. You don't. You're safe here. With me.' He planted a possessive palm over her breast, feeling its warm weight, satisfaction rising at the gasp of delight she couldn't stop.

She was his and he'd protect her.

He pressed closer, his thighs surrounding her, one arm wrapping around her, drawing her to him, while the other slipped under her top and flicked her bra undone.

'Damaso!' Her voice wasn't strident this time. She wasn't fighting him any more, *graças a Deus*. But something in her tone stopped him. Her gaze was steady and serious.

'How do you know so much about the *favelas*?'

He felt his lips hitch up in a mirthless smile. No point

denying it; she'd find out sooner or later, even if it wasn't public knowledge. 'Because it's where I'm from.'

Damaso waited for the shock to show in her eyes. The disgust.

Her hand brushed his cheek again then tunnelled through his hair, pulling his head down till his forehead touched hers.

'The place where we were today?'

Slowly he shook his head and drew another breath into cramped lungs that burned as they expanded. 'Somewhere much worse. It's long gone, bulldozed and redeveloped.'

She said nothing and with each second's silence he waited for her to pull away. Now she knew what he really was.

The opinion of others had never mattered. He'd been too busy clawing his way out of poverty to care about anything but climbing each successive step to success. But Marisa's reaction mattered.

His fingers flexed against her satiny skin, his hands big and rough against her delicate, refined body.

When she did move it took a moment to realise what she was doing. She pulled back but only to haul off her top and bra. Her summer-bright eyes held his as her clothes, a tangle of bright silk, fell to the floor.

'I'm sorry I worried you.' Her voice was high and breathless, but not as oxygen-starved as he was, watching her small hands anchor his much larger ones over her delectable breasts. The warmth of her soft body melted a little of the ice in his veins. Her nipples, firm and peaked, tickled his palms, making his breath ease out on a sigh.

His brain struggled to compute what she was doing. How had they gone from his life in poverty to this?

'You could just have told me.' Her gaze meshed with his as her hand went to the zip of his jeans.

Damaso swallowed hard, giving thanks for the strange yet wonderful impulses of his reckless princess.

* * *

Damaso drowsed at her breast, his hold encompassing her even in sleep. For the first time he hadn't demurred when she'd told him to stay where he was in the languid aftermath of love-making. Instead of rolling aside, he lay spread across her, as if melding himself with her.

For that was how their loving had felt. Slow and deliberate and possessive in a way that made Marisa's throat catch and her heart drum when she remembered it.

Yet there'd been desperation too, in his eyes and in the barely contained power of his body bringing her to ecstasy again and again.

Marisa smiled against his warm skin. She was making up for all those years of sexual abstinence. Just one of the benefits of having a lover like Damaso.

Her smile faded.

What would he be like as a husband?

For the first time she allowed herself to consider the possibility dispassionately, pushing aside her anxiety at the idea of tying herself to any man. Would Damaso be any more controlling than the unknown aristocrat her uncle wanted her to marry?

Damaso was dominant, bossy, used to getting his own way. But he'd never bullied her like her uncle, and no one could accuse him of being cold like her father. The more she knew him, the more she wondered how she'd ever thought him cold. Damaso was hot-blooded and passionate. Not just in bed; when he talked of their baby the glow in his eyes revealed a depth of feeling that had at first scared her and now... Marisa blinked. It soothed her, she realised.

She *liked* him caring so strongly for their baby. It was reassuring to know that if something happened to her Damaso would be there to look after their child.

He made her feel less alone. In the past she'd had Stefan and losing him had devastated her. That tearing hurt had made her even more determined not to open herself up to anyone. But slowly Damaso had been breaking down her barriers. Now he was *there*, firmly planted in her life, pushing the yawning chasm of darkness back till she no longer felt on a precipice of pain.

He tried to protect her too. Damaso was always at her side now at any society event.

Then there was his reaction to her visit today.

Marisa's brow puckered, remembering his stark expression when he'd spoken of the danger. She remembered the scars on his body and how he'd got them. Yet instinct told her this was about more than some physical threat.

Clearly Damaso had reacted on a visceral level. Perhaps, if she understood him, she might trust him enough to accept what he offered.

Shame bit. She'd been focused on her independence and on grappling with the changes this pregnancy would bring. She'd been self-absorbed, every bit as selfish as the press painted her.

Oh, she'd been curious about Damaso, always fascinated by the man who'd slowly begun to reveal himself to her. But she'd never pushed to delve deeper. True, he was taciturn about his past, always focusing on the here and now or the future. But she could have tried harder. He'd been genuinely sympathetic when she'd told him about herself. What had she given in return?

Damaso was inextricably part of her life now. As her child's father and more, much more.

Marisa swept her hands over his broad shoulders, marvelling at the closeness she felt, the bond that wasn't just to do with the baby but with them as a couple. She hugged him tight.

A couple. It was a new concept.

Maybe for the first time she had, after all, found a man she could trust.

* * *

Her second trip to the *favela* tested his temper but not in the way she'd expected.

'I thought we'd agreed it was too risky for you to spend time there.' He stood, tie wrenched undone at his throat, shirt sleeves rolled up to reveal strong, sinewy arms and fists buried in his pockets. His brow was like a thundercloud as he watched her from the door to the private roof-garden.

He looked vital and sexy, and something clenched hard in Marisa's stomach as she met his scowl. Kneeling as she was, she had to crane her neck to survey his long, powerful body but it was worth it. She had to scotch the impulse to go to him and let him kiss her. If she did there was a danger she might cave in rather than stand her ground. He was that persuasive.

'I listened to what you said, Damaso, which is why I agreed when Ernesto insisted on taking other guards.' Privately she thought the security precautions overkill but she'd fight one battle at a time.

'He should never have allowed you—'

'We've been over that.' She lifted one wet hand and pushed her hair off her face with the back of her wrist. 'Don't you dare bully Ernesto. He was just doing his job. If he'd tried to stop me I'd have gone without him.' It wouldn't be the first time she'd evaded professional minders.

'I was safe. And I was welcome.' The generous welcome she'd received had been heart-warming. 'I helped a little with one of the classes and talked to the co-ordinator about reviving the photography project.'

Marisa wasn't qualified to teach but knew a little about that. Enough to foster the efforts of the few youngsters who'd taken part in an earlier program to develop photography skills. The co-ordinator had talked enthusiastically about career-building. For Marisa, though, it was about helping others find the peace and satisfaction she herself felt looking at the world through the lens of a camera.

'That would mean going there regularly!'

Marisa didn't bother answering. She'd known Damaso would be angry but she was determined to proceed. For herself, because selfishly she clung to the idea she could be useful, and for the kids.

Was it preposterous to think she also did this for Damaso? For the orphan he'd been, struggling to survive in a tough environment? Who had helped him? Ever since he'd let her glimpse the pain of his past, she'd found herself imagining him on streets like those she'd walked today. Was it hardship that had honed him into the man he was—ruthless and single-minded, guarding his heart so closely?

She groped for the soap that had fallen into the basin of warm water, feeling it slippery on her palm.

'And it doesn't explain what you're doing with *that*.' Damaso's voice dropped to resonant disapproval.

Marisa surveyed the skinny dog she held by the scruff of the neck. It trembled as it stood in the big basin of tepid water but made no move to escape.

'He needed a home.'

'Not this home.' Damaso stalked across to stand over them, his long shadow falling on the pup.

'If it's a problem, I'll take him elsewhere.' She paused, more nervous than she'd expected now it came to it. She was sure of her ground, wasn't she? Yet if he called her bluff... No, that wouldn't happen. 'I'm sure I'll have no trouble finding somewhere to stay where dogs are welcome.'

The silence was so loud it reverberated in her ears.

'Is this you making a point, Marisa?'

She looked up to see him watching her through narrowed eyes.

'No one ever accused me of subtlety. But, no, it's not.

The poor thing was in need of a home, that's all. And I…'
She shrugged and lathered the dog's fur. 'It seemed right.'

She could have said more—about how she'd always
wanted a pet, about her growing desire to care for something after being so alone. But in truth she'd looked into
those hopeful, canine eyes and felt a twang of fellow feeling. Here was another outcast, someone who didn't fit and
didn't expect to be wanted.

Damaso moved closer and the dog shivered. Marisa put
out a soothing hand to gentle it.

'I can find a good home for it. It doesn't belong here.'
His offer surprised her and she jerked her gaze back up.

'Thank you.' His expression told her he didn't want anything to do with the dog. 'I appreciate it. But I want to look
after him myself.'

If she could do a good job of looking after a dog, perhaps
she could work her way up to caring for a baby. Besides,
he trusted her; she couldn't let him down now.

Damaso's gaze shifted to the dog and Marisa sucked
in her breath at the antipathy in that stare. No wonder the
poor thing was shaking.

'You can't be serious. Look at it! It's a mongrel. If you
must have a dog, at least let me get one for you from a
breeder.'

'A pure-bred, you mean?' Her hand slowed and she put
the soap down.

'Why not? Surely that's more fitting?'

'For a princess?'

'It's what you are, Marisa. There's no point pretending
otherwise.'

'Is that what you think I'm doing? Pretending to be
someone I'm not?' Hurt scored her voice. Is that what he
thought she'd been doing on her visit today?

'Of course not.' He strode away then spun on his foot.
'Just look at it. No matter what you do, it will always be a
slum-bred mongrel.'

The words echoed in her head. Marisa read Damaso's taut features, the rigidity of his big frame. She'd only seen him like this once before, when he'd been so adamant she stay away from the *favela*.

Because he was ashamed of where and how he'd grown up?

It didn't seem possible. She'd never met a man more grounded and self-assured than Damaso.

Yet he harped so often about her royal lineage, as if that mattered a scrap compared with character.

'It's probably carrying disease too.'

Marisa shook her head and reached for a bucket of rinse water. 'I've taken Max to the vet and he's had the all clear.'

'Max?'

Marisa tipped the water gently over the dog and reached for another bucket.

'He reminds me of my great-uncle, Prince Maximilian.' Despite the tension in the air, she smiled. 'Same long nose, same big brown eyes.'

Great-Uncle Max had been a scholar, happier with his books than playing politics, but he'd always had time for Marisa, even hiding her when she'd played hooky from history classes. But then Uncle Max had had a way of bringing the past alive in a way her teachers didn't.

She blinked hard, surprised to feel her eyes prickle at the memory of those brief snatches of childhood happiness.

Damaso watched her intently from beneath lowered brows, his gaze shifting from her to the dog.

'You really do care about the animal.' There was a thread of shock in Damaso's voice.

Admittedly Max, drenched and bony, wasn't the most handsome dog around, but he had character.

Marisa shrugged and finished rinsing off the soap suds. Even she was surprised at how quickly she and Max had bonded. She couldn't send him back to the streets, not now. Despite what Damaso thought, this wasn't some deliberate

test of his forbearance. It had been an impulsive decision
that she'd known instinctively was right.

'Very well, it can stay, but I don't want to see it inside.'

Damaso turned back into the apartment before Marisa
could thank him, but a tiny glow of heat flared inside and
spread. 'Hear that, Max?' She reached for the towel Beatriz had provided and began to dry him. 'You can stay.'

They'd both found sanctuary with Damaso. His reasons
weren't purely altruistic, since he was angling to convince
her to stay long-term. But Marisa had experienced enough
duplicity to know actions did count louder than words.

She wondered if Damaso had any idea how much his
generosity meant.

CHAPTER TWELVE

'THE CITY LOOKS wonderful at this time of night.'

Damaso watched across the table as Marisa leaned back in her seat, sipping from a goblet of sparkling water as she surveyed the panorama. The view from his private roof garden had always been spectacular but he'd never found time to appreciate it until Marisa had moved in with him.

There were a lot of things he hadn't fully appreciated.

His gaze roved her golden hair, loose over her shoulders, the dreamy expression in her eyes and the ripe lushness of her breasts beneath the filmy, sea-green top.

He'd known many beautiful women but none of them had made the breath seize in his lungs or his chest contract.

'I love this city.' Her smile widened.

'You do?' He raised his beer glass to his lips rather than reveal how pleased he was by her announcement. 'Why?'

She shrugged. 'It's vibrant, so different from Bengaria. There's so much happening, and the Paulistanos have such energy.' She looked at the table between them and the remains of the meal Beatriz had served. Her hand slipped to her stomach. 'Plus, I love the food. If I'm not careful, I'll be fat as butter by the time the baby's born.'

Damaso shook his head. Only a lover would know she'd put on a mere couple of pounds during her pregnancy. As that had only made her pert breasts fuller, he wasn't complaining.

He tried to imagine her swollen with his child and a stab of possessiveness seared through him.

Just as well she enjoyed the life here. He wasn't letting her go, even if she had yet to come to terms with the fact.

'My uncle has invited me to his coronation.'

Damaso stilled, fingers tightening on his glass. 'You're not going? You hate Cyrill.'

'I don't know,' she said slowly. 'At first I didn't intend to, but I'm wondering. I don't want to see *him*, but sometimes it feels like I'm hiding here, afraid to go home and face the music.' Her jaw angled higher in that determined way she had. 'I don't like that.'

He frowned. 'I thought you told me Bengaria wasn't home.'

She shrugged. 'I wasn't happy there but it's in my blood.'

'So what are you thinking? That you owe it to your uncle to hold his hand through the coronation? You want to play happy families with him?'

Marisa's mouth turned down. 'Not that. I just wondered if it wasn't better to face them all.'

'Why?' He leaned close. 'So they can lecture you about your irresponsible behaviour in getting pregnant?'

Damaso silently cursed his straight talking when she winced and looked away. Yet everything in him rose up in protest at the idea of her leaving, even for a short visit.

If she went to Bengaria, what was to stop her staying? Certainly not love for him. They had great sex, and she seemed as content as he to spend time together, but nothing she'd done or said indicated she'd fallen for him.

His pulse quickened. Was that what he wanted—Marisa head over heels in love with him?

That would solve all his problems. Marisa in love would be a Marisa committed to staying. It would hardly matter that he didn't know the first thing about love or relationships. She had enough warmth for the pair of them, the three of them.

In his bleaker moments he wondered if he had it in him to learn how to love.

'You think going back would be a mistake?'

Damaso paused, conscious that this was the first time Marisa had asked his advice.

Was it wishful thinking, or was this a turning point?

Stifling a triumphant smile, he tempered his words, cautious not to sound dictatorial like her uncle. Marisa could be persuaded, not ordered. He'd learned that quickly. Better if she thought staying was her decision.

'I think you need to consider how your uncle will try to use your presence to his advantage. Do you want to be his dupe?'

The tightening of her lips told him he'd struck a chord. Marisa was proud. She wouldn't want to play into the hands of a man she despised.

'Why don't you decide later?' Damaso knew better than to push his advantage. 'Tell me about your day,' he urged. 'I haven't seen you for hours.'

There was another first. He looked forward to their evenings together, discussing the day's events. It was something he'd never experienced with anyone else.

'I took the kids to the gallery.' She leaned forward, her eyes shining, and he congratulated himself on hitting on something to take her mind off Cyrill. 'You should have seen how excited they were. Silvio spent a couple of hours with them and they drank it all in.'

'I'm sure they did.' He remembered the first time he'd left the neighbourhood where he'd grown up. The excitement and fear. The children Marisa had taken under her wing with her photography classes would never have dreamed of anything as plush as Silvio's gallery. As the most successful photographer in South America, and probably beyond, he could name his own price for his work.

'I have to thank you for introducing me to him.' Marisa's hand found his and he threaded his fingers through hers, marvelling again at how something so delicate and soft could be so strong. 'I've admired his work for years, but…'

'No need to thank me.' They'd been over that weeks ago, when Damaso had taken her to Silvio's gallery. She'd been in seventh heaven, so rapt in Silvio's artwork that the photographer had taken an immediate shine to her. They'd been thick as thieves ever since.

Damaso might have been jealous of the way Marisa spoke so often of Silvio, except it was his work she was interested in, and her responsiveness to Damaso was unabated.

Anything that strengthened Marisa's ties to Brazil, such as her friendship with Silvio, was something Damaso encouraged. Besides, watching her enthusiasm as she talked about how her young photographers had blossomed at this rare opportunity was like watching a flower open to the sun.

Something stirred and eddied in his chest as a smile lit her face.

She was so happy.

It was only now, seeing her excitement, hearing her enthusiasm, that he realised how she'd changed. She'd always seemed vibrantly alive. But now Damaso knew her well enough to recognise that in the past some of her vivacity had been a persona, like clothing worn to project an image.

Damaso knew about that. In the early days he'd acted the part of successful businessman even when he'd had barely enough money to feed himself. He'd poured everything into becoming the man he was determined to be. Convincing others to trust him had been part of that.

Seeing Marisa glow from within, he realised the woman he'd met in the jungle had been going through the motions, despite her bright, engaging smile. Grief had muted her.

The real Marisa was stunning, almost incandescent. The sort of woman to draw men, like moths to flame.

He'd never felt as lucky as he did now, despite the niggle

of doubt, because she hadn't yet agreed to marry him. His hand tightened on his beer and he took another swallow.

'Silvio offered to meet them again and look at their work. Isn't that fantastic?'

'Fantastic,' he murmured. 'But they're already learning a lot from you.'

Marisa's sessions with the kids had been a huge success. He'd heard from a number of sources how enthusiastically not only the teens but their parents too had responded, plus he'd seen the results.

Marisa shook her head. 'I'm an amateur.'

'A talented amateur.'

'Flatterer.' Her eyes danced and again Damaso felt familiar heat in his belly.

It still unsettled him, knowing Marisa was going to the *favela*. He wanted to lock her away so she couldn't be hurt. But seeing her now, he knew he was right to hold back.

Movement at the end of the table caught his eye as the mongrel dog sidled up to her chair. With a fond glance, Marisa reached down and stroked its head, then tickled it under the chin. The dog closed its eyes in ecstasy and leaned closer.

Damaso's mouth thinned. What did she see in it? Watching her delicate fingers ruffle its fur just seemed wrong. He could give her a dog bred specifically to be a perfect companion. Instead she settled for a ragged mongrel that looked like it belonged on the streets, no matter how much she bathed and brushed it.

Marisa caught the direction of his stare.

'Why don't you like him?' Marisa's head tilted to one side in that characteristic look of enquiry.

Damaso shrugged. 'I don't have time for pets.'

Her silence told him she didn't buy that.

'But it's not just any pet, is it? You offered to get me another dog to replace him.' She paused, studying him carefully. 'It's something about Max.'

Damaso said nothing. He'd agreed to let the animal stay. What more could she want?

'It's because of where he comes from, isn't it?' She leaned across the table. 'Is that why you can't bear to look at him?'

Marisa sank back in her chair, her fingers burrowing deep into Max's fur as understanding hit out of the blue.

She'd been in Damaso's island home, and here in his city penthouse, and only now realised that, while he didn't display his wealth with crass ostentation, everything was of the highest quality materials and craftsmanship.

Nor had she seen anything with the patina of age— no antiques, nothing second-hand. Everything was pristine, as if it had been made yesterday. Many of the pieces had been created by world-renowned artisans, from the artwork to the furniture, and of course the architectural design of the buildings.

The same applied to his luxury hotel in the Andes. Only the best, nothing ordinary or even old.

Terrible foreboding tingled down Marisa's backbone and she straightened, putting down her glass. She put both hands on the table, as if to draw strength from the polished metal.

'What is it?' No fool, Damaso had picked up her sudden mood change, from curiosity to stomach-curdling distress.

'Everything you own is top of the range, isn't it? Only the absolute best.' Even the kitchen where Beatriz presided would do a Michelin-starred restaurant proud.

'What of it? I can afford it and I appreciate quality.'

'Quality.' The word tasted bitter. It had been a favourite of her uncle's, especially when he berated her for mixing with the 'wrong' sort of people.

Marisa swallowed hard, telling herself she was mistaken. Yet nothing could dispel the suspicion now it had surfaced.

'Marisa? What is it?' Damaso's brows drew down in a

frown that, instead of marring his features, emphasised their adamantine charisma. 'There's nothing wrong with owning beautiful things.'

'It depends why you want them.'

For long seconds she fought the sickening idea, but it was no good. Finally the words poured out. 'Is that why you're so insistent marriage is our only option?'

His eyes widened. 'What are you talking about? I don't see the connection.'

'I come with a pedigree. Having a royal title means I'm *quality*.' She dragged in a breath that didn't fill her lungs and stared into his expressionless features, looking for some sign she was wrong.

'You think I'm hung up on a royal title?'

Marisa pressed her palms harder into the cool metal of the table.

'I know you want my baby.' How stark the words sounded, crashing through the truce they'd built so painstakingly. Yet she couldn't shy away from the truth. 'But maybe there's more to it.'

Inside a voice cried that she was wrong. That Damaso was different. But how could she trust her judgement on this? She'd been wrong before.

'What do you mean?' He sat so still she knew he exercised steely control.

'Your reaction to me visiting the *favela* is out of proportion to the danger, especially given the bodyguards you insist on.' Something flashed in his eyes and her heart dived. 'I think the reason you don't like Max is because he comes from a slum.'

Marisa paused and waited but Damaso said nothing. The only animation was the tic of a pulse in his clenched jaw.

'Tell me the truth, Damaso.' She sucked in an unsteady breath. 'Do you want me as a trophy to add to your collection? After all, a princess comes pretty close to the top of the heap if you care for titles and *quality*.' Try as she might, she couldn't stop herself gagging on the word.

She'd thought she knew Damaso, that they shared something fragile and precious, something that made her happier than she could ever remember being. She'd begun to trust him, to hope.

'If you want to hide from your past and pretend it never happened, saddling yourself with me isn't the way to do it. Remember, most people don't think of me as a quality item. I'm sullied goods.'

'Don't talk like that!' He lunged across the table, his hand slamming down on hers, holding her captive. His dark eyes sparked, as if she'd tapped into a live volcano. 'Don't ever say such things about yourself.'

Marisa tried to look down her nose at him. She'd learned the trick from her haughty uncle and it had proven invaluable when she'd wanted to hide private hurt. But it didn't work now. Somehow she'd lost the knack—or Damaso had burrowed too far beneath her defences.

Desperation added an edge to her voice. 'Why not? It's what everyone thinks, even if they don't say it to my face. You might consider me the royal icing on the cake of your success, something special to add to your collection.' She swept a glance beyond the exquisite hand-forged table and chairs to the sculptures scattered through his private garden that would have done any national gallery proud. She gulped, her throat raw. 'But I'm flawed, remember? That detracts from my value.'

He moved so fast, her head spun. Large hands cupped her cheeks, turning her head up to where he towered above her.

'Don't ever say that again.' He bit the words out, his face drawn as if in pain, his eyes furious. Oddly, though, his hands felt gentle against her chilled flesh. 'I won't have it, do you hear? You're so wrong.'

Damaso looked down into her wide, drenched eyes and

had never felt so furious or helpless. Why couldn't she see what he saw? A woman worthy of admiration and respect. A woman unlike any he'd known.

Marisa blinked, refusing to let the glittering tears fall. It was typical that even now she put on a show of pride.

Yet the reminder of her vulnerability tore through him. Damaso dropped to his knees beside her seat, only vaguely aware of the dog darting out of the way.

He felt as if something had broken inside him when he saw her hurting so badly.

Leaning close, he drew in the familiar scent of green apples and sweet woman. Every instinct clamoured for him to haul her to him and make love to her till he blotted all doubt from her mind. But she needed to hear the words.

He swallowed hard. 'You've begun to believe your uncle's lies.' He saw her eyes widen. 'He's always put you down, tried to restrict you and mould you, but you didn't let him. You were too strong for that. Don't let him win now by undermining your confidence.'

Damaso paused, letting her digest that.

'For the record, any man would be proud to have you as his wife. And not because of your royal blood. You're bright and caring, not to mention beautiful. You're intelligent, fun and good company. You must have noticed how everyone wants to be with you.'

It was painful to watch the doubt still clouding her eyes. 'You know how much I want you, Marisa.' He grabbed one of her hands and planted it on his chest so she could feel the way his heart sprinted.

'You want my baby,' she said slowly. 'But do you want me or the cachet of marrying into royalty? If social status is important, that would be some achievement for a boy from the slums.'

'I want us to be a family.' The words rumbled up from some place deep inside. *Family.* The strength of his need for Marisa and their child undid him. 'I want to be with our child and I want to be with *you*. You know that. You felt the chemistry between us from the first.'

'You mean the sex?' She breathed deep and he had the impression she had to force the words out. 'People don't marry for that. What other reason could you have?'

Damaso looked into those brilliant, guarded eyes and realisation slammed into him. He'd seen that yearning look before, years ago, when he'd broken off with a lover who'd begun to want too much.

Perhaps Marisa didn't know it, but it was emotion she craved from him. Shunned by her family and her country, Marisa needed love.

A lead weight plummeted through his gut.

Marisa wanted the one thing he didn't know how to give.

For a moment he thought of lying, trotting out the trite words that would salve her pain. But Damaso couldn't do it. She'd see straight through the lie and convince herself it was for the worst possible reason.

Panic rocked him. He'd do so much for her. Anything except let her go.

He had nothing to give her except the truth.

Damaso reached for her hand and closed his fingers around it. Her other hand was still plastered against his chest. Did she notice how his heart raced?

'You think I surround myself with beautiful things to escape my past?' He drew a harsh breath and forced himself to go on, ignoring a lifetime's instinct for privacy. He had to share what he'd hidden from the world or risk losing Marisa.

'You could be right,' he said eventually and heard her hiss of indrawn breath. Her hands twitched in his and he tightened his hold implacably, refusing to let her pull away. He stroked his thumb over hers where it rested on his chest.

'I started with nothing but the clothes on my back.' He grimaced. 'I was determined to shake off the dust of what passed for my home as soon as I could. By sheer hard work and some very lucky breaks I succeeded and, believe me, I never once looked back with regret. As soon as I could, I surrounded myself with the trappings of success. Sharp clothes, swanky office, beautiful women.'

At Marisa's expression he smiled, buoyed a little at what he hoped might be jealousy. 'Why wouldn't I? I'm only human.'

'I'm not judging.'

He shrugged. 'I'm not ashamed of enjoying success. My priority was always to plough back profits into the business and have enough capital to optimise any opportunity. That's how I moved from running errands to being a tourist guide and then owner of a tour company. We became known for delivering the best vacation experiences, taking people to places others couldn't or wouldn't.

'As the profits grew, my interests spread across a range of ventures. I'd always had a taste for clean clothes and comfortable housing and saw no reason not to indulge myself.'

He watched Marisa digest that. 'Along the way I developed an interest in modern art, possibly from visiting so many galleries. When I got money, I bought pieces I liked. Just as I bought cars and houses that appealed.'

Damaso paused, remembering her accusation. 'I'd never considered it before but you're right. I prefer to own beautiful things. I feel no need for external reminders of where and how I grew up. I'm surrounded by others who share similar memories, even if we don't speak of them.'

Marisa was silent for a moment. 'Ernesto?'

Damaso nodded. 'And Beatriz. All my personal staff. I didn't know them when I was a kid, but they come from similar places.'

'No wonder they think the world of you. You've given them the chance they needed.'

He shrugged. It was easy to lend a hand when you had

his advantages. Marisa made it sound like he was some sort of saviour of the slums.

He thought of her dog, rescued from a similar place, and winced. Marisa had hit the nail on the head. Whenever he looked at her petting that mutt, it highlighted the gulf between her and him: the refined princess and the rough-and-ready slum kid.

'Damaso? What is it? You're holding me so tight.'

Instantly he eased his grip. But he didn't let her go. Anxiety clutched his belly. He'd never spoken about his childhood. But if he wanted to keep Marisa…

'You think I can't bear to be reminded of where I came from, but I carry it in my bones.'

He wanted to leave it at that but Marisa needed more. At the same time, he realised this wasn't just about easing her fears. She'd cared enough to wonder about his past, not just now, but before this. How many had done that?

Pleasure and horror surged.

'Tell me.'

He let her hands go and stood, turning towards the city vista.

'I barely remember my mother and I have no idea who my father was. I didn't have a real home. I lived…' He swallowed and forced himself to go on. 'You've seen photos of ragged kids scavenging on garbage heaps? That was me.'

Suddenly he was there again, the odours pungent in the rain, the ground slippery mud and worse beneath his feet, his saturated clothes sticking to his skinny body.

Damaso felt movement and realised she'd come to stand beside him.

'Later there were charity hand-outs, but my main memory is the pain of an empty belly. All day, every night.' He blinked and the images before his eyes resolved into the downtown cityscape.

Marisa's hand slipped into his and his fingers closed around it. Strange how good that touch felt.

'You think I overestimate the danger for you. Maybe I do.' The admission cost him. Every instinct urged him to keep Marisa and their child away from there. 'But where I grew up...' He lifted tight shoulders. 'I saw too much violence to take safety for granted.'

'Those knife scars,' she said, her voice soft.

Damaso nodded. He refused to tell her the details of gang rivalries, drug dealing and more. 'I saw death up close too often. I was lucky to get out when I did. A lot of kids didn't. The neighbourhood you visit is much safer than mine, but something inside me screams out every time you go there.'

'I'm sorry.' She leaned against him, her weight warming his side.

'But you still want to help those children.' His mouth twisted. He hated her being there but how could he be anything but proud and moved that she wanted to help?

'You think I'm being selfish?' Her face turned up to his and he read her doubt.

'I think you're a wonderful, warm-hearted woman and I want you in my life.' He turned and put his arms around her, pulling her close.

'Really?'

'Absolutely. Your social status and bloodline never mattered to me. I take people as I find them— rich, poor or in between.' He lifted her face so she looked into his eyes. 'I want you for purely personal reasons and I don't give a damn what anyone else thinks. Understood?'

For long seconds she watched him silently then she stood on tiptoe and whispered against his mouth. 'Understood.'

The look in her eyes made his heart swell.

CHAPTER THIRTEEN

'YOU LOOK STUNNING.' Damaso surveyed her appreciatively. From the top of her golden head to her jewelled stilettos, she was perfection.

Covertly he searched for some evidence of her pregnancy but even after several months she still appeared trim and taut. He looked forward to the day when it would be obvious she was pregnant.

Possessiveness raked familiar talons through his insides. He didn't want to share Marisa. He wanted to keep her with him, away from the men who slavered after her wherever she went.

'Why, thank you.' She twirled, her multi-coloured dress flaring high, revealing toned legs, lightly tanned and delectable. His groin tightened as he thought of some of the things he'd prefer to do with the evening.

But this was her night.

'I have something for you.' His voice was gruff. He told himself that just because she'd refused to accept anything but hospitality from him didn't mean she'd refuse this. He reached for the slim leather case on the bedside table. She was so stubbornly independent, who knew how she'd react?

Damaso forced a smile, feeling tense muscles stretch. What was wrong with him? He'd given women gifts before, casually lavish presents that had meant little.

But this wasn't casual. This he'd chosen personally, had had it designed specifically for Marisa.

He watched her eyebrows arch as she recognised the distinctive logo of one of the world's top jewellery designers.

'There was no need.' She made no move to reach for it and a cold feeling invaded the pit of his stomach.

'I know.' He held her eyes but for the first time in weeks had no idea what she was thinking. Had the closeness between them been a mirage?

'You admire so many Brazilian designers, I thought this would appeal. When I saw it I thought of you.' It was true. No need to reveal his long consultation with the designer about Marisa and her style.

He proffered the box and after a moment she took it. Heat swirled through him in a ribbon of satisfaction.

She didn't open the gift immediately but smoothed her hand over the embossed emblem. Finally she lifted the lid and he heard the snatch of her indrawn breath.

For long seconds she said nothing, eyes fixed on the contents, lush lips slightly parted. Then her throat worked.

Had he miscalculated? Got it wrong?

Eyes as brilliant as the summer sky met his. The way she looked at him made him feel ten feet tall.

'They're absolutely gorgeous.' The catch in her voice tugged at something inside and Damaso wanted to reach out and gather her close. He told himself to wait. 'I've never seen anything like them.'

That was exactly what he'd wanted, because he'd never met a woman like her. 'You like them?'

'*Like* them?' She shook her head, her expression bordering on dazed. 'They're fabulous. How could anyone not like them?'

'Good, then you can wear them tonight.'

Was it his imagination or did she retreat a fraction?

'Why, Damaso? Why the expensive gift?'

He stared down, willing her to accept. 'You deserve to celebrate your first public exhibition. The cost is immaterial; you know I can afford it.'

'Not *my* exhibition.' Despite the doubt in her eyes, her lips curved slightly. 'Tonight is about the kids' photography.'

'Not according to Silvio. From the way he talks, he has big plans for you.' Damaso watched as delicate colour washed her cheeks. 'As well as for your class.'

'So it's a congratulatory gift, because you think I should celebrate?'

Damaso hesitated, reading her anticipation. She wanted more but what could he say? That seeing her contentment and purpose had made him happier than he could ever remember?

That he wanted to keep that and keep *her*?

That he wanted to put his ring on her finger and bind her to him?

He'd had enough of waiting and battled not to behave like an unreconstructed male chauvinist, forcing her to stay despite her doubts.

'You've worked hard and achieved so much,' he said at last. 'You're making a difference to those kids, giving them skills and confidence and using your connections to open up a new world to them.'

'Really?' It didn't seem possible but Marisa's eyes shone brighter.

He nodded, his throat closing as he saw how much his words meant. Marisa was so active and energetic, sometimes it was easy to forget the burden of doubt she struggled with.

'As an up and coming photographer, you need to look glamorous at your premiere.'

'Looking the part, then?' Her eyes dropped and Damaso reached out and tilted her chin up. Her soft skin made his fingers slide wide, caressing her.

'Far more than that, Marisa. I…'

She leaned towards him and he had the sudden overwhelming conviction she was waiting for him to say something deep, something about how he felt.

Damaso swallowed, knowing he was on dangerous ground.

She'd become a vital part of his future, her and the baby. They brightened his world in a way he'd never thought possible. Yet if he blurted that out her beautiful mouth would thin and she'd turn away.

'I'm proud of you, Marisa. You're a special woman and I'd be honoured if you'd wear my gift tonight.'

Something that might have been disappointment flickered in her eyes then she nodded, but her lips curved in a smile. Damaso assured himself he'd misread her.

'Thank you. I'd like that,' she said huskily.

He reached into the open box and took out the necklace, letting the fall of brilliant burnt-orange gems spill across his palm.

'They remind me of you,' he murmured, watching the light catch them. 'Light and colour and exuberance, but with innate integrity.' He looked up to find her wide gaze fixed not on the strands of gems but on him.

'Really?'

He nodded and moved behind her, drawing the ends carefully together around her throat. 'Absolutely.' Quickly he fastened the clasp and drew her across to a full-length mirror. 'They're pure summer, just like you.'

'What are the stones?' She sounded awed, as well she might. A frisson ran through him at how perfect they looked on her—how perfect she looked, wearing his gift.

'Imperial topaz, mined here in Brazil.'

Marisa lifted a hand to her throat then let it drop, her eyes wide as she stared at the necklace. From its wide topaz-and-diamond collar, separate strands of faceted topaz fell in an asymmetrical cluster to just above her cleavage. It was modern, sexy and ultra-feminine. Just like Marisa.

'You're the most beautiful woman I've ever seen.' At least he could admit that truthfully.

Predictably she opened her mouth as if to protest, but Damaso reached around her and pressed a finger to her siren's mouth.

'Put the earrings on.'

Silently she complied.

'And the bracelet.' A moment later diamonds and topaz encircled her slim arm and Damaso wrapped his arms around her and drew her back against his chest, watching their reflections in the long mirror.

'You like them? You're happy?'

Marisa nodded silently, but her eyes glowed.

He told himself that was enough for tonight. He'd been right to hold the ring back instead of proposing. But time was running out. He refused to wait much longer to claim her.

Marisa's cheeks ached from smiling. Ever since she and Damaso had stepped off the red carpet and into Silvio's soaring studio, she'd been accepting congratulations for her work and for the youngsters she'd been mentoring.

Silvio had been brilliant with the kids, letting them bask in the positive reception their work received without letting them be overwhelmed. One success, he'd warned them, didn't build a career. But hard work and application would.

Now, for the first time in what seemed hours, she found herself alone with Damaso amidst the buzzing, sophisticated crowd. His hand closed on hers and her heart took up a familiar, sultry beat as she looked into his gleaming eyes.

She was hyper-aware of the weight of his jewellery at her throat and wrist, a tangible proclamation of his ownership. That was one of the reasons she'd resisted accepting his gifts. He was a man who'd take a mile when offered an inch. She'd clung to her independence with the tenacity of a drowning man grabbing at flotsam as he went under for the last time.

Yet what was the point in pretending? It wasn't the jewellery that branded her as Damaso's but her feelings.

When he'd presented her with the exquisite pieces she'd been on tenterhooks, waiting for him to announce they were a symbol of what he felt for her. She'd hoped his feelings for her had matured miraculously through sexual attraction, admiration, liking and caring to…

A shiver rippled across her skin.

'Come on,' she urged before he could guess her thoughts. 'There's one piece you haven't seen, at least not blown up to this size.' Threading her fingers through his, she tugged him towards an inner room.

Damaso lowered his head, his mouth hovering near her ear, his breath warm on her skin. 'The portrait of me?'

Marisa nodded and kept walking, the jittery, excited feeling in her stomach telling her she was in danger of revealing too much to this perceptive man.

They stopped on the threshold of the room and, as luck would have it, the spectators parted so they had an unhindered view.

The tingling began somewhere in her chest and spread out in ever-widening ripples just as it did every time she saw it. The photographer in her saw composition and light, focus and angle. The woman saw Damaso.

Not the Damaso the world was used to—the fiercely focused businessman—but a man she'd only just discovered. The slanting light traced his features lovingly in the black and white shot, revealing the broad brow, strong nose, the angle of cheekbone and jaw and the tiny lines at the corner of his eyes. But it did more. It captured him in a rare, unguarded moment, hunkering down with a dark-haired little boy, bent over a battered toy truck.

The man in the photo leant protectively close to the tot, as if to shield him from the football game that was a blur of action on the uneven dirt behind them. His eyes were on the boy and his expression...

Marisa swallowed. How had she ever wondered if Damaso would make a good father? It was all there in his face: the intense focus on the child; the protectiveness; the pleasure lurking at the corners of his firm mouth as he solemnly helped the boy fill the back of the truck with dirt scooped from the earth at their feet.

Damaso would make a wonderful father; she knew it in her bones. Since being with him her doubts about her ability to be a good mother had receded too. His praise and his trust did so much for her. His steady presence had even helped her to find a purpose.

'Thank you for agreeing to let me hang this one.' Her voice was husky and she had to work to counter the urge to press her palm to the tiny swell where her belly sheltered their child.

Beside her, Damaso shrugged. 'You and Silvio were so adamant it had to be included. How could I refuse?'

'I—'

'How fortunate to find you here, princess.'

Marisa's head jerked around at the interruption, her hackles rising at the deliberate emphasis on her title. Her stomach dropped as she recognised the country's most notorious art critic, an older woman renowned for her venom rather than her eye for talent. They'd met at a high-profile event where they'd had opposing views on the merit of a young sculptor.

The woman's cold, hazel eyes told Marisa she hadn't forgotten, or forgiven.

'Damaso.' She turned. 'Have you met—?'

'I have indeed. How are you, Senhora Avila?'

'Senhor Pires.' The woman's toothy smile made Marisa shiver. 'You're admiring the princess's work?' Again that emphasis on her title. 'I hear Silvio is quite taken with his protégée.' Her gimlet gaze and arch tone said she couldn't see why. 'That he's even considering taking her on as an assistant!'

Fed up with being spoken about as if she wasn't there, Marisa simply pasted a smile on her face. If this vulture wanted details, let her pump Silvio. Knowing how Silvio despised the woman, she wouldn't get far.

When the silence lengthened the woman's face tightened. 'Of course, there are some who'd say social status is no replacement for real talent. But these days so much of the art scene is about crass commercialisation rather than true excellence. Anything novel sells.'

Her dismissive attitude scored at something dark inside Marisa. The belief that beneath her determined bravado her uncle had been right. That she had nothing of value to offer.

Dimly she was aware of Damaso squeezing her fingers.

She caught herself up. She'd let doubts undermine her too long. No more. She opened her mouth to respond but Damaso was quicker.

'Personally I think anyone with real discernment only has to see these works to recognise an amazing talent.' His tone was rich, dark chocolate coating a lethal blade. 'As for milking social status, I don't see any reference in the studio or the catalogue to the princess's royal status.'

Beside her he loomed somehow taller, though she hadn't seen him move. 'I suspect those who gripe about social status are only hung up on it because they're not happy with their own.'

Marisa bit back a gasp. It was the sort of thing she'd often longed to say but had never felt free to express.

'Well!' Senhora Avila stiffened as if she'd been slapped. Her eyes narrowed as she took in Damaso's challenging stance. Finally she looked away, her gaze sliding to the photo.

'I must say, Senhor Pires, this piece paints you in a new light. You look quite at home in that slum.' Her eyes darted back to him, glittering with malice. 'Could it be true, after all? The whisper that that's where you came from? No one seems to know for sure.'

Marisa stepped forward, instinctively moving to block the woman's venom. She knew how raw and real Damaso's past was to him, even now. His hand pulled her back to his side and she leaned into him as his arm circled her shoulders.

'I don't see why my birthplace is noteworthy to someone whose interest *purports* to be in art.' His tone lowered the temperature by several degrees. 'It's true I grew up in a *favela*. What of it? It wasn't an auspicious start but it taught me a lot.'

He leaned towards the woman and Marisa saw her eyes widen. 'I'm proud of what I've done with my life, Senhora Avila. What about you? Can you name something constructive you've done with yours?'

The critic mouthed something inarticulate and spun on her heel, scuttling away into the crowd beyond.

'You shouldn't have done that,' Marisa murmured. 'She'll blab to the whole world what she's learned.'

'Let her. I'm not ashamed of who I am.' He turned her towards him, his gaze piercing, as if the glamorous throng around them didn't exist. 'Are you all right?'

'Of course.' Marisa stood straighter, still shaken by the force of anger that had welled when the woman had turned on Damaso.

Because Marisa loved him.

There, she'd admitted it, if only silently. She'd fought so hard against the truth, acknowledging it was a relief. Marisa hugged the knowledge to herself, excitement fizzing through her veins.

She felt as if she could take on the world.

'You should have let me answer for myself. I'm not some dumb bimbo, you know.'

His mouth curled up at one corner. That smile should be outlawed for the way it made her insides melt.

'You? A bimbo?' He laughed and she had to fight the urge to lean closer. 'As if.' His expression sobered. 'But you can't ask me to stand by while that viper makes snide comments about the woman I intend to marry.'

Was it her imagination or did the crowd around her ripple in response to that low-voiced announcement?

'Not here, Damaso!' Suddenly she wanted more than anything to be alone with him. She longed for the privacy of his city penthouse or, even better, his island hideaway. 'Let's talk at home.'

The promise in his sultry stare sent her heart fluttering against her ribs. He looked like he wanted to devour her on the spot. Even his public assertion that he intended to marry her, something that would once have raised her ire, sent a thrill of excitement through her.

Yet it was another hour before they could leave, an hour of accolades that should have meant everything to her. Instead, Marisa was on edge, her mind reeling as she finally confronted her true feelings for Damaso. She wanted him…permanently.

The one thing she didn't know was what he felt for her. He'd publicly revealed his past to deflect that critic's spite. A past he'd once guarded jealously.

At last they were in the limo. Marisa couldn't sit still. Adrenalin streamed through her body, making it impossible to relax. She wanted to blurt out her feelings but what would that achieve? He famously didn't do relationships. Just marriage for the sake of his child.

But surely the way he'd stood up to that harpy meant something?

Something as impossible as him loving her?

The idea shimmered like a beacon in the distance, filling her heart with hope.

Even if he didn't love her, Marisa couldn't resist any

longer. She'd marry him anyway. She'd never meet a better man than Damaso, or a man she cared about more.

She wanted to spend her life with him.

A weight slid off her shoulders as doubt was banished. She wanted love, she'd fight to get it, but she'd start small if she had to. Surely she could make him love her in time?

She was so engrossed in her thoughts she barely noticed him talking on his phone until he spoke to her.

'It's bad news, Marisa. A fire in the new Caribbean eco-resort.'

'Is anyone hurt?'

'They're checking now. It's too early to say. But I need to go there tonight.'

Marisa reached out and wrapped her hands around his tight fist. She knew how much worker safety meant to him and this new complex, due to open in weeks, had been the focus of his attention for so long.

'Of course you should go. You've invested too much time and effort not to.'

'I'll be gone a week, probably more like two. You can come with me. I don't like leaving you alone.'

'I'll hardly be alone.' She shook her head. 'You'd get more done without me and I have lots of work to do too, remember? Silvio and the kids are relying on me.'

Besides, it struck her that she had other unfinished business.

She'd used Damaso's opposition as an excuse to stay away from her homeland. Yet increasingly she'd known she had to face her past just as Damaso had faced his.

Her past took the form of her uncle and the Bengarian court and press. Staying in Brazil, pretending the coronation wasn't happening, felt too much like hiding, as if she was ashamed of who she was and what she'd done.

If she didn't stand up to them, how could she hold her head high?

Marisa was determined to become the woman she wanted

so badly to be—not just for herself but for Damaso and their child. For Stefan too. She'd make them proud.

She wanted to be strong the way Damaso was. The past was part of her, but she had to prove to herself she wasn't cowed by it.

Besides, she had to be stronger now than ever before. Enough to take the chance and stay with a man who had never said he loved her and who might never say it.

Marisa swallowed hard, trying to ignore the fear crawling down her spine.

She'd go to the coronation, face her past and reconcile the two parts of her life. Maybe then she'd be the sort of woman Damaso could love.

'Marisa? What is it? You have the strangest expression.'

She turned, her emotions welling unstoppably. 'Don't worry about me,' she urged. 'Just go. I'll be fine while you're away. I'll be busy.'

She needed to do this alone.

CHAPTER FOURTEEN

HIS TWO WEEKS in the Caribbean had felt like two months. More.

Damaso jabbed the button for the penthouse and shoved his hand through his hair. He needed a haircut. He rubbed his chin, feeling the rasp of stubble, and knew he should have shaved on the plane. But he'd still been working frantically, trying to get everything organised so he could come back a couple of days early.

He'd shave when he got to the apartment.

Except he knew once he saw Marisa his good intentions of sparing her delicate skin would fly out of the window. There would be no holding back.

He needed her *now*.

He needed her in ways he'd never needed a woman. His arms felt empty without her. He missed her smile, her sassy challenges, the sly way she teased him, the fearless way she stood up to him. He missed having her nearby, sharing the small stuff from their days he'd never thought important before he met her.

The doors opened and he strode into the apartment.

'Marisa?'

Long strides took him past the vast sitting room to their bedroom suite. She wasn't there. He headed back down the corridor.

'Marisa?'

'Senhor Pires.' It was Beatriz, wiping her hands on an apron. 'I didn't expect you back yet.'

'I changed my plans.' He looked past her for Marisa. Surely she'd heard him by now. 'Where is the princess?'

Beatriz stilled, her brows lifting. 'She's gone, Senhor.' Damaso felt his blood turn sluggish, as if his heart had slowed. 'Back to Bengaria for the coronation.'

Damaso rocked on his feet, absorbing the smack of shock. He'd spoken to Marisa daily and she'd said nothing about leaving.

Because she feared he'd stop her?

It was the only explanation.

That last night at the exhibition he'd mentioned marriage and she'd tried to hustle him away. Because she'd decided to leave him?

'Senhor? Are you all right?'

Damaso shook his head, trying to stop the sick feeling surging through him. He reached out and splayed a hand against the wall, grateful for its solidity.

'Can I get you—?'

'Nothing,' he croaked. 'I don't need anything.'

Except Marisa. Hell! It felt like the world crumbled beneath his feet.

Heedless of Beatriz's concerned gaze, he stumbled back to the bedroom.

Fifteen minutes later Damaso slumped on the bed. He'd tried her phone but it was switched off. He'd checked his email—nothing. He'd even accessed her personal email, something he'd never before stooped to doing, and found nothing relevant.

There was no note, no message. Nothing except, in the drawer of her bedside table, a crumpled letter from her uncle. A letter demanding her presence for the coronation. A letter that spelled out the importance of Marisa returning to meet the man her uncle intended her to marry.

Bile rose in Damaso's throat as his gut knotted.

She'd left him and gone to her uncle, the man she abhorred.

Because she'd rather marry some blue-blooded aristocrat than Damaso, a man without a family tree to his name? A man whose only pretensions to respectability had been bought with his phenomenal success. A man who still bore scars from his slum background.

He'd have sworn that didn't matter to Marisa. But, if not that, then what?

Unless, like him, Marisa had doubts about his ability to be a father. To provide love.

How could you give what you've never known?

Fear gouged his belly, scraping at his deepest, most hidden self-doubt.

Something nudged his knee and he slanted his gaze down. That ragged mutt of Marisa's leaned against him, its chin resting on his leg, its eyes soulful in its ugly face.

The dog's coat felt surprisingly soft under his fingers. Its huge eyes narrowed to slits of pleasure as Damaso stroked one torn ear.

'You miss her too, don't you, Max?'

Strangely, it seemed completely natural to talk to the dog. It leaned close, its weight warm and comforting.

Surely she'd have taken the mutt if she'd intended leaving for good?

That shard of hope gave him strength.

'Don't fret.' Damaso straightened his spine. 'I'm going to get her back, whatever it takes.' He refused to dwell on whether he spoke to reassure the dog or himself.

The cathedral was huge and impressive. Damaso barely gave it a glance as he stalked up the red carpet, ignoring the usher frantically trying to catch his attention.

The atmosphere was expectant and the air smelt of massed blooms, expensive scent and incense. Baroque organ music swelled, lending pomp to the occasion.

Damaso slowed, surveying the crowd. He saw uniforms and dark suits on the packed seats, clerical robes and women in designer dresses. But the hats the women wore obscured profiles and made it impossible to identify the wearers till they turned and stared.

'Princess Marisa,' he barked to the usher. 'Where is she?'

'The princess?' The man's gaze flicked nervously up the centre aisle to the front seats. Instantly Damaso strode away, leaving the goggling man behind.

Heads whipped around as he passed but he looked neither right nor left as he scanned the front rows. Pale blue, lemon, ivory, that light shade of brown women insisted on giving names like 'beige' or 'taupe'. His stare rested on each woman then moved on, dismissing them in turn. White, pink, more pink, light grey. They were dressed expensively but sedately. Obviously there was a book of etiquette on what to wear for a coronation: expensive but subdued.

Damaso shifted his gaze to the other side of the aisle. Grey, black, and…deep sapphire-blue swirled with an orange so vivid it reminded him of the sun blazing on his island beach at sunset. He faltered, his heart pounding.

He'd found her.

Instead of a suit she wore a dress that left the golden skin of her arms bare. She looked like a ray of light amidst the sedate pastels. She moved her head and the jaunty concoction of orange on her golden hair caught the light. It looked saucy even from behind.

His pace lengthened till he stood at the end of the row and he caught the full impact of her outfit. Elegant, but subtly sexy in the way the fabric hugged her curves. At her throat she wore the magnificent topaz necklace and for a moment Damaso could only stare, wondering what it meant that she'd chosen to wear *his* gift to an event that would be televised to millions.

The murmurs became a ripple of sound around him. The usher had caught up and was whispering urgently about the correct seating.

Still Marisa didn't turn. Her attention was on the man sitting on her far side. A man with a chiselled jaw, wide brow and face so picture-book handsome he didn't look real. Or maybe that was because of the uniform he wore. His jacket was white with gold epaulets, a double row of golden buttons down the front, and he sported a broad sash of indigo that perfectly matched his eyes.

Damaso's fists curled. Was *this* the man she was supposed to marry?

Far from spurning him, she was in deep conversation with the guy. He said something and she leaned closer, her hand on his sleeve.

Something tore wide open inside Damaso. Cold rage drenched him as his fists tightened.

'Sir, really, if you come with me I'll just—'

'Not now.' His voice was low, almost inaudible, but it had the quality of an animal growl. The usher jumped back and heads whipped round.

'Damaso?' Marisa's eyes were wide and wondering.

She'd forgotten to remove her hand from Prince Charming's sleeve and Damaso felt a wave of roiling fury rise up inside him.

Marisa stared up at the man blocking the aisle. Despite his formal clothes, his perfectly cut hair and clean-shaven face, there was something untamed about him.

Emotion leapt. A thrill of excitement, of pure delight that Damaso was here.

'How did you get here?' Cyrill wouldn't have invited the father of her unborn child.

'Does it matter?' Damaso shrugged off a couple of ushers who were trying to lead him away. He looked broad and bold and impossibly dangerous, like a big jungle cat caged with a bunch of tabbies.

Silently she shook her head. No, it didn't matter. All she cared about was the fact he was here. Her heart tilted and beat faster.

He held out his arm, palm up. 'Come on.'

Marisa stared. 'But the coronation! It's due to begin in a couple of minutes.'

'I'm not here for the coronation. I'm here for you.'

Her pulse fluttered high in her throat at the command and possessiveness in his voice. She prized her independence but his proprietorial attitude spoke to a primitive yearning within.

Behind her, women leaned close, fanning themselves.

'Marisa?' Alex spoke beside her. 'Do you want me to deal with this?'

Before she could answer, Damaso stepped close, shoving aside an empty chair into the path of a uniformed man who'd reached to restrain him.

'Marisa can speak for herself. She doesn't need *you*.' She'd never heard Damaso sound so threatening. His eyes flashed pure heat and there was violence in his expression.

'Damaso. Please.'

'Please what? Go away?' Those hot eyes turned to her, scorching her skin and sending delicious chills rippling through her tummy. 'Not a chance, *querida*. You don't get rid of me so easily.'

'It's not a matter of getting rid—'

'We need to talk, Marisa, *now*.'

'After the ceremony.' She gestured to the fallen chair. 'I'm sure we could arrange for you…'

Damaso's eyes cut to Alex and his look was downright ugly. 'If you think I'm leaving you with him…' He shook his head. 'I know you don't want to be here, Marisa. Don't let them force you.'

Marisa frowned, trying to make sense of his attitude.

Then Alex surged to his feet and so did Marisa, arm out to separate him from Damaso.

'Stop this now,' she hissed. 'You're making a scene, both of you. Everyone's watching.' Yet part of her revelled in Damaso's single-mindedness.

'Are you coming with me?' His accent was thicker, enticing, like rich coffee laced with rum. It slid along her senses, beckoning.

'Damaso, I don't know what this is about but I—'

A swoop of movement caught the rest of the sentence in her throat. Next thing Marisa knew, she was in Damaso's arms, held high against his chest. On her peripheral vision, she saw a television camera turn to focus on them. A babble of sound erupted.

'Marisa.' Low, urgent, Alex's voice reached her. She turned her head and saw him just inches away, scowling, as if about to tackle Damaso. He had no idea she'd rather be in Damaso's arms than anywhere. She groped for Alex's hand, squeezing it quickly.

'It's okay, really,' she whispered. 'I'm fine.' And then his hand slipped from hers as Damaso swung round, stalking through the protesting crowd to turn back up the long aisle.

Perhaps the tabloids were right—she was lost to all propriety. Rather than being outraged by Damaso's scandalous behaviour, Marisa found herself thrilled at his masculine display of ownership. Hope rose.

He *must* care for her.

No man would behave so outrageously unless he cared. She was sure that was jealousy she'd seen glinting in the basilisk stare he'd given Alex.

'You could just have phoned,' she murmured, snuggling closer to his solid chest.

His firm stride faltered and he looked down at her. 'Your phone was off.' A ferocious scowl marred his brow and beneath it his eyes were shadowed by something that looked like doubt. 'You didn't tell me you were coming.'

Marisa frowned and lifted her hand to his face. His skin was tight and hot.

'I thought you'd follow me if I told you.'

His nostrils flared and his jaw set as he looked away and started moving again, shouldering his way through the clustering crowd. 'You wanted to be alone to meet the man your uncle has arranged for you to marry.'

'You know about that?' To her amazement, she still had the capacity to feel shock.

'Isn't that why you came? To get engaged to some pretty-boy aristocrat who doesn't give a damn who you really are? Who doesn't even care you're carrying another man's baby?'

Marisa heard the gasps around them but only had eyes for Damaso. What she read in his face outweighed any annoyance she might have felt for his careless words. She read *pain*. The sort of pain that tore at the heart and shredded pride.

She should know. She'd seen the symptoms in her own face when she'd faced a future loving a man who cared only for their baby.

How it hurt to see Damaso suffering too.

His big body hummed with tension. His jaw was set so hard she wondered how he'd ever unclench it.

'I won't let you do it. He's not the man for you, Marisa.'

'I know.' Her voice was so soft she thought at first he hadn't heard. Then he juddered to a halt, his head jerking round. The intensity of that midnight gaze transfixed her.

'You know?' His voice was muted roar. She'd never seen a man so close to the edge. Her heart clenched. Could it be true? Could the miracle she'd hoped for have happened?

'I'm not here to choose a fiancé.' She planted her palm on Damaso's chest, feeling the racing rhythm of his heart. 'I'm here because I'm a princess of Bengaria. I have a right to be at the coronation, as well as a duty. This is my country, even if I don't plan to live here full-time.'

'Where do you plan to live?' His low voice was barely audible, yet the echo of it rolled across her flesh, raising shivery goose bumps.

'Brazil looks nice.'

Marisa felt the jolt of shock hit him. His hands tightened as his head lowered to hers.

Dimly she was aware of a distant camera flash.

'You're not trying to leaving me then?'

She shook her head, her throat closing, as for the first time she saw right to his soul. Longing, pain and determination were there, plain for her to see.

'You'll marry me.' It was a statement, not a question, but Marisa nodded.

'Why?'

The question floored her. From the first, he'd been the one demanding marriage. Had he changed his mind? Her stomach swooped. 'I could ask you the same thing,' she whispered.

'Why do I want to marry you?'

She nodded again, aware that this wasn't the best place for this conversation. But nothing, not protocol or natural disaster, would have stopped her now. She had to know.

A slow movement started at the corner of his mouth, pulling it up in a crooked smile that grew till it carved a dimple down one cheek and broadened into a grin. It transformed Damaso's face from hard and determined to charismatically sexy. Marisa's heart missed a beat.

'Because I want to spend the rest of my days with you.' He lifted her in his arms till his words were an invisible caress on her parted lips. His dark gaze locked with hers, promising a gift far more precious than any regal entitlement. 'Because I love you.'

She blinked but still couldn't take it in. 'Say that again.'

This time Damaso lifted his head and when he spoke his words rang through the crowded cathedral for all to hear. 'I love you, Marisa, with all my heart and soul. I want to be your husband, because there's no woman in the world more perfect for me than you.'

He loved her?

Marisa felt the hot glaze of tears film her eyes as emotion welled from deep within. A sob rose, turning into a hiccup of desperate happiness. Never in her life had she felt like this.

'Now, *meu anjo,* tell my why you want to marry me.' His gaze dropped to her belly and she knew he was thinking of their child.

She shook her head. That wasn't the reason.

'Because I love you too, Damaso. I love you from the bottom of my heart and I couldn't bear to be with anyone else.'

Beyond them the sophisticated crowd went wild.

'I've been in love with you so long,' she whispered, drawing him closer, her words for his ears only. 'It feels like I've only come alive since I've been with you.'

Finally Damaso spoke, his voice uneven, his eyes glittering. 'Do you really want to stay for the ceremony, since you came all this way?'

'I'd rather be with you, Senhor Pires. Take me home.'

Marisa had thought his last smile potent but this one was enough to stop clocks. Two ladies-in-waiting swooned as Damaso tucked her against his heart and strode down the aisle.

'And they accuse *me* of being scandalous! Your behaviour was outrageous.'

Damaso smiled at the lush, lovely woman sitting in the jet's private lounge, sipping sparkling water.

Marisa was his. Incontrovertibly, absolutely *his*.

Something smacked him hard in the chest. Relief? Triumph? Joy? He didn't give a damn what name it went by. It was the best feeling in the world. He felt like he might burst with happiness.

'Your uncle will get over it,' he murmured, sitting down beside her, one hand on her thigh. The whisper-thin silk of her dress was warm from her flesh, inviting further exploration.

'I doubt it. The look on Cyrill's face when you told him I couldn't stay for the ceremony because I had another engagement! I thought he was going to have a seizure.' She shook her head. 'Upstaging him at his own coronation! Such lack of decorum.'

Marisa looked down as his hand slipped higher up her leg but did nothing to stop him. 'At least that will have dashed any plans he had to marry me off.'

'You wouldn't have been happy with that pretty-boy aristocrat.' Only he could give her what she needed, for he was the one she loved. He'd never known love. It took some getting used to.

'Of course not.' She leaned forward and he was momentarily distracted by a glimpse of delicious cleavage.

'He didn't even have the gumption to stop me.' Satisfied, he ran his fingers lightly up to her hip, feeling her shiver under his touch.

His.

'You mean Alex?' Her brow puckered. 'He's not the man Cyrill wanted me to marry. He's a friend.'

'I thought you didn't have any friends in Bengaria.' Despite everything, jealousy stirred. Just how close a friend was this Alex?

She shrugged. 'Okay, more Stefan's friend than mine. I haven't seen him for years. He's been away. And, no.' She paused, studying his face. 'He's not the man for me.'

'But I am.' He intended to make sure she remembered it, and rejoiced in it, every day for the rest of her life.

'You definitely are.' She lifted her hand to his cheek and an incredible peace descended as she feathered a touch across his skin. 'I'm a better person with you, Damaso. I feel...proud of what I've done and what I'm doing. Confident about the future. You gave me the strength to face what I'd been running from.'

'You were strong before you met me, Marisa.' He'd never known a woman more feisty and independent.

She shook her head. 'It was only when I saw how you'd faced your past and got on with your life that I realised I'd been a coward, letting Cyrill and the press drive me from my home. That's why I had to go back. To prove to them, and to myself, that I'm happy with who I am. I mightn't fit their mould but that doesn't matter.'

'You're perfect just the way you are.' His hand strayed to her abdomen and the baby bulge that had popped out in the two weeks since he'd seen her. His palm closed protectively over it. His woman. His child.

Marisa shifted, her eyes skimming away from his. She took a swift sip from her glass.

'What is it?' Instantly he sensed her discomfort. 'What's wrong?'

She lifted one shoulder. 'Nothing. Everything's perfect.'

Yet her smile wasn't quite as radiant as it had been. Damaso tilted her head around till she had no choice but to meet his scrutiny. 'Something's bothering you. Tell me.'

One slim shoulder lifted. 'No, really, I—'

'Don't, Marisa. You've never lied before. Your honesty is one of the qualities I admire most. Tell me the truth. If there's anything wrong, we need to work it out together.'

Eyes of bright azure locked with his, her regard so searching it was as if she looked deep into him.

Damaso looked right back. He had no secrets from Marisa.

'I *like* that you're so eager to be a father.' She paused, giving him time to process the doubt in her voice.

'But…?'

A flush coloured her cheeks. 'But…' She bit her lip, reminding him of the early days on his island estate when she'd refused his offer of marriage. She hadn't thought a child sufficient reason to marry.

'But you're afraid it's our baby I want,' he murmured. 'Rather than you.'

She opened her mouth to answer but his finger on her lips forestalled her.

'I love our child already, *meu anjo,* and I'll work hard to learn to be a good father.' He swallowed hard, knowing that would be a bigger challenge than any corporate dealings. 'But, even if there was no child, even if there could never *be* a child, I would love you with my whole heart.'

Marisa's eyes shone brilliantly as she looked up at him. He took the glass from her hand and set it down, then gathered both her hands in his. They trembled. Or perhaps it was he who shook.

'You are my sun and stars and moon, Marisa. You've taught me how to care about more than a balance sheet. That it's not my corporate empire that defines who I am. It's who I love.'

He raised her hand and kissed it, revelling in the fresh apple and sunshine scent of her skin, knowing it would always be his favourite perfume.

'I didn't know I *could* love till until you came into my life.'

Her eyes glittered with tears but her smile was the most wonderful thing he'd ever seen.

Damaso dropped to his knees in front of her. 'Will you be mine? We don't need to marry if you—'

This time it was Marisa's finger on his mouth.

'I'll marry you, Damaso. I want everyone to know you're mine.' Her smile was incandescent. Damaso felt its warmth in every cell of her body. 'Besides, for a scandalous princess, I have a hankering for respectability, so long as it's with you.'

'Ah.' Damaso rose and lifted her into his arms, turning towards the luxuriously appointed bedroom. 'That's a shame. I was rather hoping for a little scandalous behaviour now and then.'

Marisa reached out and with one quick tug undid his bow tie and tossed it over his shoulder. Her smile was pure seduction. 'I'm sure that could be arranged, Senhor Pires.'

* * * * *

MILLS & BOON®

Maybe This Christmas

Author of *Sleigh Bells in the Snow*

Sarah
Morgan

Maybe
this
Christmas

COMING SOON
OCTOBER 2014

* cover in development

Let Sarah Morgan sweep you away to a perfect
winter wonderland with this wonderful Christmas
tale filled with unforgettable characters, wit,
charm and heart-melting romance!
Pick up your copy today!

www.millsandboon.co.uk/xmas

MILLS & BOON®

Why shop at millsandboon.co.uk?

Each year, thousands of romance readers find their perfect read at millsandboon.co.uk. That's because we're passionate about bringing you the very best romantic fiction. Here are some of the advantages of shopping at www.millsandboon.co.uk:

✷ **Get new books first**—you'll be able to buy your favourite books one month before they hit the shops

✷ **Get exclusive discounts**—you'll also be able to buy our specially created monthly collections, with up to 50% off the RRP

✷ **Find your favourite authors**—latest news, interviews and new releases for all your favourite authors and series on our website, plus ideas for what to try next

✷ **Join in**—once you've bought your favourite books, don't forget to register with us to rate, review and join in the discussions

Visit **www.millsandboon.co.uk**
for all this and more today!